KU-365-020

The Haunting
of Houses

By the same author

Elizabeth the Beloved
Kathryn, the Wanton Queen
Mary, the Infamous Queen
Bride for King James
Joan of the Lilies
Flower of the Greys
The Rose of Hever
Princess of Desire
Struggle for a Crown
Shadow of a Tudor
Seven for St Crispin's Day
The Cloistered Flame
The Woodville Wench
The Peacock Queen
Henry VIII and His Six Wives
Jewel of the Greys
The Maid of Judah
The Gallows Herd
Flawed Enchantress
So Fair and Foul a Queen
The Willow Maid
Curse of the Greys
The Queenmaker
Tansy
Kate Alanna
A Child Called Freedom
The Crystal and the Cloud
The Snow Blossom
Beggar Maid, Queen
I, The Maid
Night of the Willow
Ravenscar

Song for a Strolling Player
Frost on the Rose
Red Queen, White Queen
Imperial Harlot
My Lady Troubador
Lackland's Bride
My Philippa
Isabella, the She-Wolf
Fair Maid of Kent
The Vinegar Seed
The Vinegar Blossom
The Vinegar Tree
Lady for a Chevalier
My Catalina
The Noonday Queen
Incredible Fierce Desire
Wife in Waiting
Patchwork
Minstrel for a Valois
Witch Queen
Much Suspected of Me
Proud Bess
The Flower of Martinique
England's Mistress
A Masque of Brontës
Green Apple Burning
Child of Earth
Valentine
Child of Fire
Verity
Trumpet Morning

The Haunting of Houses

MAUREEN PETERS

ROBERT HALE · LONDON

© Maureen Peters 2006
First published in Great Britain 2006

ISBN-10: 0-7090-8021-2
ISBN-13: 978-0-7090-8021-3

Robert Hale Limited
Clerkenwell House
Clerkenwell Green
London EC1R 0HT

The right of Maureen Peters to be identified as
author of this work has been asserted by her
in accordance with the Copyright, Design and
Patents Act 1988

2 4 6 8 10 9 7 5 3 1

MORAY COUNCIL LIBRARIES & INFO.SERVICES	
2O 18 83 53	
Askews	
f	

Typeset in 12/15½pt Baskerville
by Derek Doyle & Associates, Shaw Heath
Printed in Great Britain by St Edmundsbury Press
Bury St Edmunds, Suffolk
Bound by Woolnough Bookbinding Limited

For Geraldine Casimir, a keen student of the Brontës, who from time to time flees from her domestic duties to roam Yorkshire with me, and whose informed help and enthusiasm during the writing of this novel have been invaluable.

ONE

September 1802

An hour since, after a coach ride from Liverpool that ground my bones into splinters, I arrived here in the market town of Gimmerton, and reserved a room at a shabby but decently clean hostelry.

The inn stands at the top of a steep, narrow main street, and is of the millstone grit I have recently seen through the windows of the coach as we wended a way past dreary houses before which lines of washing strung across front yards flapped in the stiffening breeze.

The road itself turned and twisted, now needling its way through streets, now swooping down into valleys where autumn tinted trees crowded together, and I glimpsed the silvery brown of rushing water, now rising higher towards bare crags and sweeps of yellowing grass and dark sliminess of peat.

I longed to be on board ship again, gripping the rail and watching the white billows as the vessel rose and sank and my fellow passengers, none of whom I knew, retched and heaved below decks. But I am bound by promise to come here into the north, and so I am come.

The room I was ushered into is comfortable enough with a good feather mattress on the bed and an eiderdown as multi-coloured as the coat Joseph wore in the Bible. There is a fire burning now in the grate but the ashes were being raked out when I stepped in and the landlady, a plump good-humoured woman, insisted on showing me downstairs into a snug parlour tucked behind the public bar where she brought hot coffee and a great pie filled with pieces of beef and carrots and potatoes, together with a loaf of white bread and an apple tart with a glazed roof.

'Eat hearty, Miss Stewart, and your chamber'll be ready in a trice!' she encouraged, so I have eaten heartily, and now, having washed the travel dust out of my face and hands and combed my hair I am seated at a table in a high-backed chair with inkwell and blotter and my own pen and journal before me.

I have written in the journal at intervals since my grandfather gave it to me when I was eight years old. It has a red cover and on the flyleaf, penned in his flowing hand, it reads:

Aspen Stewart

Her Book

Below the inscription pressed flat against the paper is a four-leaved shamrock.

'The faces of God,' my grandfather told me when we found it one afternoon. 'The Father for Power, the Son for Love, the Spirit for Inspiration.'

'And the fourth one?' I wanted to know.

'The Female for the Hidden Mysteries,' Grandfather said and would explain no more.

I did not write in it then, but kept it for a year, pressing the four symbols of God below my grandfather's hand. A year later my own childish scrawl first appeared.

'Grandfather died. My father came.'

Grandfather had been ailing for some time though I, being young, noticed only that he took longer to mount his horse and that, after darkness fell, he would seem tired and sometimes a little peevish, which was rare with him for he'd a sweet temper.

Then on my ninth birthday everything changed though I didn't realize it fully until I was much older.

I had gone across the parish boundary into the district of Drumballyroney, which is separated by an imaginary line from Imdel where our own lands are held. What physical divisions exist are scattered along the border in the shape of glen and tumulus and bits of broken wall. The Bruntys hold land there though whether by right or arrangement with their McClory cousins I never knew for certain.

It was a soft green September day with the sun hung like a ball of gold above the glens and the corn standing tall for the reaping. I rode Jackdaw, my pony, having saddled her myself and led her past the sleeping groom. Grandfather had promised to ride with me but after the midday meal he had fallen into a doze by the fire and I had grown weary of waiting and left the room quietly, determined to have my ride whether he came or not. I had no fear of a scolding for Brigit had gone to have a tooth drawn and would be absent until evening.

Some of the Brunty children were in the field that adjoined their house, the boys bowling an iron hoop between the stocks of corn while their sisters tumbled in the long grass that sloped towards the glen. I saw Hugh, who was taller than the rest and my elder by a few months, and James, who was seven, and Welsh, who was only five and little and dark unlike his siblings who were all fair. The two older boys were at work, Pat labouring for the village weaver and William helping out at the blacksmith's.

Jane stopped playing as I arrived and sat up with her skirts spread about her like the petals of a white flower stained with pollen from the corn dust. Usually she was with her mother and something inside me hurt when I saw them because my own mother died when I was born, or a few days later.

'Milk fever,' Brigit said. 'It carries off many mothers.'

And I saw milk fever as a white horse with mane and tail of cream and young mothers in white nightgowns flung over its back.

Ellis wasn't there that afternoon and Welsh, who was always the first to give tongue, shouted to me, 'Mam has a new baby girl!'

'Named Mary!' Hugh supplied, tossing down his hoop and running to where I had drawn rein.

'How do you know?' I asked.

'Because mother said,' Hugh told me.

He had reached up to grasp the pommel of my saddle and his eyes were bright blue under his thatch of light reddish hair. My hair is dark but it has a red sheen on it and Grandfather used to tease me and say that I had caught it from the Bruntys.

'I'd like to see her,' I said, but he shook his head and stood away, eyeing me with his head on one side as if he measured something.

'You might put the evil eye on her,' James piped up.

'I will not!'

'You might! Uncle Paddy told as how your dadda came out of the darkness and laid a spell before he rode away again,' Hugh said.

'That's a lie, Hugh Brunty!'

I lashed out with my whip and caught him a beauty across the face which set him howling with fury.

That was when a man on a black horse did canter down the green slope, using his bigger whip to lash the Bruntys aside.

'I'll tell dadda!' Welsh shrieked.

'You tried to kill us!' James complained, picking up Jane who clung round his neck sobbing.

'Not one of you is touched,' I said scornfully, holding my own mount in check along with my fear. 'Run home and tell tales if you like but don't blame me if you get a whipping for telling lies!'

They scattered along the glen, Jane still hanging on to James, Welsh lingering to send us a long thoughtful glance before he too leapt away.

'And what,' the stranger enquired, fixing me with brooding black eyes, 'was that all about?'

'Private business,' I said haughtily.

The Bruntys might be annoying but they were compatriots of mine and most of our encounters were good humoured.

'Private, eh?'

He went on looking at me for a moment and there and then he began to laugh, sharp white teeth glinting in a sallow, gypsy-ish countenance.

He was darkness coming out of darkness, I thought, and think now. Riding coat and breeches of sombre hue, the narrowest of white stocks, and black hair tied back with dark ribbon. On one long, tanned finger an oddly twisted ring of greyish-white showed against the darker skin as he peeled off his riding gloves and laughed.

'You must be Aspen,' he said at last.

'Aspen Stewart, sir,' I said politely, determined to be the lady. 'And you are—'

'None of your business,' he answered coolly. 'My business is with your grandfather. Is he at home?'

'Yes. What business?' I enquired. 'Grandfather tells me many things about the farm and the crops and livestock. He says that it will be mine one day when he is gone to heaven.'

'Does he, by God? That will make for an interesting topic of conversation,' he said.

'I am riding home myself,' I volunteered, having just decided. 'I can show you the way.'

'I know the way,' he said. 'They've not moved the house in the last nine years, I daresay?'

'No, of course not!'

I giggled at the notion of our big old house being lifted up and set down in another place.

'Don't smirk,' he said curtly. 'If there's anything I cannot abide it's a smirking, swooning ladylike creature. So today is your birthday?'

'Yes, but how did—?'

'You ask too many questions. You'll be wanting a present I suppose?'

'Not from a stranger,' I said.

'Ah, but we met before,' he returned. 'Your grandfather and I are old . . . friends.'

I thought that unlikely because in my childish ignorance I could not imagine an elderly gentleman like Grandfather being close friends with a man who looked to be a few years short of thirty.

'I will be glad, sir,' I said hesitatingly, 'if you did not tell my grandfather that I am riding alone.'

'Ah! We break rules, do we?' He laughed again. 'I will say nought and you will take this as a gift.'

He edged his horse nearer and took the greyish-white ring from his little finger, taking my hand and pushing it on to my middle finger.

'What is it made from?' I heard myself asking as I turned it loosely on my finger, seeing the delicate twisting spirals with their dark specks engrained in the grey-white.

'Bone,' he said, and pressed my hand so hard that the ring, loose though it was, dug into my finger. 'I set a cage of fine mesh once over a nest of baby lapwings until they starved to death because the parent birds could not get near to give them food. I showed her the nest of tiny skeletons and she made me promise never to harm a lapwing again. I never have but I made the ring to remind myself. It is very fragile.'

He let go of my hand then and wheeled his own horse around to set it galloping up the slope again.

The sun was setting but I could see very faintly the outline of someone who rode behind him on the saddle, not touching him but seeming to my bewildered gaze to hover there like a drawing etched upon the air. Then he was gone and the glen was still again save for the whispering of the wind in the long grass as if secrets were being shared among a host of invisible beings.

Brigit always insisted the glen was haunted.

'It was once the home of the Sidhe, the Beautiful Ones,' she told me. 'If ever an ugly babe is born to them they steal a pretty human babe and leave their child in the human family, and sometimes the human mother doesn't even notice.'

'And they still live in the glen?' I asked her.

'The Sidhe are long gone,' Brigit said, with a little sigh as if she regretted their passing. 'But other beings wander there now. They say ghost fires can be seen on certain nights, burning the furze but in the morning when the people go to look not a blade is singed.'

"They say" was one of Brigit's favoured expressions. She used it whenever she couldn't give proof of her stories.

If the dark stranger had arrived to see my grandfather then it would be on a matter of business, I reasoned, dismissing Brigit's tales from my mind, and that meant that my absence would go the longer unremarked, unless the stranger mentioned having seen me. I thought he probably would say nothing but would forget me and the gift he had made me very quickly.

Yet the glen had suddenly lost its inviting aspect, had become filled with shadows that didn't reflect any of the real trees and bushes in that long, broad, grassy hollow, so I slid from the saddle and began the slow walk back home, Jackdaw loitering on the rein to munch the odd mouthful of sweet September grass.

I was within sight of the neat stone house where the Bruntys lived when Mr Brunty emerged from the front door and hailed me.

'Now will you not be coming in to see the new babe?' he asked, coming to me as I paused. 'She's to be Mary after the Blessed Virgin.'

'I'm on my way home,' I told him.

'Taking the long road, I see.' He nodded in his pleasant fashion and stood regarding me, his sandy head tilted towards me.

'Grandfather has a visitor,' I said.

'So my own just told me. A tall dark man on a black horse?' I nodded.

It seemed to me that his expression altered and hardened as if some stray unpleasantness had brushed his mind. Then he said, 'Step in and see the babe anyway. Ellis is sitting up and looks as pretty as a picture.'

Ellis Brunty, Hugh's wife, was always pretty. As tall as her husband, she had fair hair that hung in shining strands to her still neat waist and her eyes were harebell blue with long lashes tipped with gold.

I sometimes wondered if she wasn't one of the Sidhe herself but Brigit said not – she was one of the McClory clan with a tribe of red-haired brothers and there'd been trouble about her marrying Hugh Brunty who had no living relatives of his own, but the pair of them had run off to be wed and her brothers had forgiven them long since.

She was in the more comfortable of the two downstairs rooms, propped up against linen pillows with the new baby in her arms. There were fresh rushes laid over the floor and a bright fire burning in the hearth and she sent me her sweetest smile as Mr Brunty prodded me inside.

'Didn't I say now the day wouldn't be complete unless Miss Aspen arrived to see the babe?' she demanded of her husband.

'Not in my hearing you didn't,' he answered, with a wink at me. 'So what do you think of her then? Bonnie, isn't she?'

She looked to me just like any baby with a fine fuzz of light hair and eyes squeezed shut against the light.

'She's beautiful,' I said.

'A friend for Jane and more girls to follow, please God!' he was saying now. 'Ellis has a habit of making boys but a few daughters will gladden my heart.'

'Don't look to have it gladdened for at least another three years,' Ellis said drily, but her look was tender.

'And Mary is a beautiful name,' I added, remembering my manners.

'So is Aspen,' she said.

'My father named me so. Brigit told me.'

'As to that . . .' Mr Brunty hesitated before he went on. 'There was a tall, dark stranger in the glen bound for the Stewart place not long since.'

'Not—?'

I saw her eyes flicker towards me.

'Who knows?' He shrugged slightly. 'The lads said a man scared them a little while ago.'

'But they're in safe?'

'Upstairs, reading the text that Pat set them – some English book. And it's never our brood he'll be wanting!'

'Not—?'

Again the swift look, as swiftly withdrawn.

'We have oatcakes ready,' Ellis Brunty said in a voice that sounded a fraction too bright. 'Shall you have one with honey and a glass of buttermilk, darling?'

I nodded again, feeling a rumble begin in my stomach.

'Where's Timothy?' Mr Brunty asked, going over to the table

to unwrap an oatcake and spooning honey on it.

'Asleep,' I admitted.

'You rode out alone? Your grandfather would be angry if he knew,' he chided. 'Eat your oatcake and drink your milk and, in a little while, I will ride back with you.'

So I sat in the warm room and ate the cake and drank the thick sour curds of milk and the Bruntys looked at me kindly, yet with a fretfulness in their expressions that I felt but didn't understand.

'It's my birthday today,' I volunteered.

'Why so it is,' Ellis Brunty said.

'I'm nine.'

'And tall for your age!' her husband said approvingly.

'Aye, your grandfather is a good height,' Ellis Brunty said.

'My mother. . . ?' I hesitated, looking from one to the other.

'She was small and had reddish hair,' Ellis Brunty said at last. 'Hugh, darling, will you not be escorting Miss Aspen home soon? Mr Stewart will worry about her now that twilight's upon us.'

'You think I should?' Hugh was looking at his wife.

'I think it's not for us to meddle in other folks' affairs,' she said firmly, and opened the flap of her gown for the babe to feed as if that put an end to further discussion.

'Aye, maybe,' he said, opening the door and ushering me out.

'I'll bring something for the baby soon,' I promised as I went out.

I would have preferred to stay and find out more about my mother. Grandfather never spoke of her and all Brigit had ever told me was that her name had been Rosina and she had died when I was born. I had seen her grave in the church at Imdel not far from the old fort. It had a lid of stone with a carved angel at each corner blowing a trumpet and I had sometimes wondered if on the Last Day the angels would leap into life and blow their trumpets and my dead mother would find the stone too heavy to lift.

Jackdaw was still munching the grass, only raising her head reluctantly when Mr Brunty lifted me to the saddle.

'We'll go at a walk,' he said, taking the rein. 'By now your grandfather's business will be concluded for sure.'

I said nothing partly since I guessed that he had held me back a while in his house so that the dark stranger would be gone when I arrived home, partly too because he loved his family and was proud of Ellis with her fair sweetness and her brood of younglings.

Yet I still asked as we moved up the side of the glen, 'The dark man who frightened the children, did you know him?'

'I've seen him before, years ago. Now hold on tight or you'll be over her head and me getting into the devil of a lot of trouble for not taking proper care of you.'

He took long strides and the distance was not great but his strides were slow and it was on the furthest edge of daylight with the moon struggling through clouds when we reached the main gates. I could see lights flickering in the lower windows and Brigit stood on the drive, a shawl about her head and her hand shielding the flame of a lantern.

'Mr Brunty, is that you?' She came forward eagerly, her tone anxious.

'Aye, mistress, with your nursling safe and sound!' Mr Brunty answered heartily. 'She's been with us admiring the new babe.'

'She's to be called Mary,' I said, sliding from the saddle and turning to bob my thanks to my escort.

'God bless the both!' Brigit said. 'Both are well?'

'Fit as fiddles!' he answered heartily. 'Good eve to you both.'

He whistled and our stableboy hurried to take Jackdaw while Brigit hastened me in through a side door that led into the passage which separated kitchens from living rooms and the main staircase.

'Is grandfather angry?' I whispered, looking towards the study door.

'The master's talking business,' Brigit said. 'Now you must come upstairs and change your shoes and your frock for they're all over grass stains I'll be bound. Riding off like that! Mother of God, but anything might have happened!'

'Well, it didn't,' I said sensibly. 'Is grandfather talking to the tall dark man?'

'You saw him?'

We had gained the upper landing and she paused, her voice dropping to a whisper as she said, 'Now, Miss Aspen, that man's a bird of ill omen and the less you see of him the better! You go into your room now and I'll bring you some cake and milk. And keep quiet for we'd not want to disturb the gentlemen.'

I would have liked nothing better than to disturb the adults but I also wanted my cake and milk, so I went meekly in and shut the door and sat on the window-seat that overlooked the drive.

The casement was slightly ajar and when I pushed it further I could hear voices coming from the open window of the study below. The words were indistinguishable one from another but there were two voices arguing, the brogue of my grandfather gruffer than the smoother tones of his visitor.

Then Brigit entered with my light supper, and bade me shut the window before the night owl flew in, and told me that my grandfather would likely want to see me after the visitor had gone.

The next thing I heard was the clattering of hoofs down the drive and Brigit, who was turning down my bedcovers and muttering about the lateness of the hour, said she'd slip down and see if grandfather was ready to see me.

She was gone such a long time that I began to grow weary

18

and to rub my forehead against the chilly panes of the window for the curtains were not yet drawn. I blinked myself awake as more hoofbeats sounded, two riders in great coats alighting from their saddles and hurrying into the house.

Perhaps Brigit had forgotten her errand and was gossiping in the kitchens with the servants. I felt a little flame of indignation spark in me because it was, after all, my birthday and everybody seemed suddenly to have forgotten it, so I tidied my hair and started down the stairs.

Dr Drummond was just emerging from the study with Mr Alistair who was our lawyer, though I wasn't sure then exactly what he did.

When they saw me they stopped and then Dr Drummond said in a jocular tone that didn't match his grave expression, 'It's very late for little girls to be out of their beds! You run along back upstairs and I'll send your nurse to tend you.'

'I want to see grandfather,' I said stubbornly. 'It's my birthday and I haven't—'

'Your grandfather isn't feeling very well,' Dr Drummond began, but with a child's quick intuition I read his real meaning and my legs gave way forcing me to sit down on the step and grip the coils of the balustrade.

'Is grandfather dead?'

'Gone to be with the Lord,' Mr Alistair said.

'But it's my birthday,' I heard myself say stupidly. 'I am nine years old today and soon it'll be tomorrow and my birthday gone.'

Brigit bustled out of the rear quarters, wiping her eyes with the edge of her apron, and before the door swung shut behind her I heard the first keening of those servants who slept in the house.

'You come upstairs with me, Miss Aspen,' she said tearfully. 'Tomorrow you shall see your grandfather laid out neatly ready for the burying. There's a lot to be done before then, so be a good girl and come with me, there's my darling.'

I didn't want to be Brigit's darling at that moment. I wanted to be grandfather's darling and be seated on his knee and wished a happy birthday, but a child of nine has little power and I got up and went up the stairs again with my nurse sobbing behind me.

In the morning she dressed me in a neat black frock and tied my hair with black ribbon and took me by the hand into the parlour where the laying-out table stood. There was a coffin on the table and grandfather lay inside with a white sheet up to his chin and his beard jutting stiffly upward.

It didn't really look like grandfather at all and when I stood on tiptoe at Brigit's bidding to kiss his forehead it didn't feel like grandfather either but like something cold and waxy.

Though we weren't Catholics there would be a wake to please our neighbours and those of our staff who were and for the next three days the parlour seemed to be perpetually thronged with people, all in their best suits and frocks, many bearing gifts of fruit and meat and cheese.

I was kissed and petted and wept over and even in my sadness began to feel quite important.

Mr Brunty arrived, a black band round his arm, his hat in his hand and his face newly shaved and there was a great stir of interest among those already there for Hugh Brunty was known in our district as a great storyteller and wizard of words.

He kissed my hand and went over to the coffin and stood for a moment looking down at the figure within, and then his voice rang out in the imploring tones of a man deprived of that which he cherishes above all else.

'Ah, Ronald Stewart! So you are gone to your rest with not one thought for the friends you leave behind you! Were you weary of our company that you fled to the skies so soon? Did you not think of your granddaughter who stands here bereft, her garments heavy with mourning, and her only nine years old? Will you not open your eyes and return to us? Will you leave this world where you were so honoured and loved for a cold place in the starhung heavens? Ronald Stewart, Ronald Stewart, was it not enough that you deserted the land of your birth to dwell among us? Must you play the fugitive yet again? Were we not generous to you? Did we not help you in the days when the harvest was poor? Did we not grieve with you when your own darling wife died? And grieve again when your only daughter fled to heaven as her babe was born? Open your eyes and greet us again one last time!'

His voice was heavy with sorrow and accusation until I felt that grandfather might well rise up and announce he'd changed his mind about dying after all. And though I wanted him with me again my heart beat fast and something in me dreaded the idea of that waxy figure sitting up and greeting us all.

'So your mind is set upon heaven then?' Mr Brunty said in mournful tones that set some of his hearers sobbing afresh. 'Then give our loving wishes to your wife and daughter. Tell them to pray for us and tell them your granddaughter, Aspen, who knew neither grandmother or mother and whom you left without farewell, will be treated by all here with the very greatest and most loving affection. Farewell, Ronald Stewart!'

There were cries of admiration and applause as he finished and in the corner our local fiddler struck up a tune. Mr Brunty took my hand and walked with me to the open front door, seating himself on the topmost step and pressing me down beside him.

'Ellis didn't come since she's still weak after the birthing,' he told me. 'I'm sorry for your loss, darling. But you know there are many here to look out for you and look after you, don't you?'

I would have answered him but the sound of hoofbeats up the

drive stopped me. On that still September day I think I knew
who had just arrived.

The tall stranger brought a darkness into the day, though he
was a handsome man with the strong planes of his face and the
high-bridged nose and the dark eyes beneath the black brows.

'So the old man left all to his granddaughter?' he said.

'I believe so,' Mr Brunty said.

He had risen to his feet but he didn't match the other's height
even when he descended to two steps above him.

'You believe so! Your name is written as witness to the will,'
the dark man said. 'Alistair told me, kindly gave me a copy! The
old devil kept me from the estate then as he once threatened he
would?'

'Do you blame him?' Mr Brunty asked.

'Blame him!' The other gave a sneering chuckle that somehow made the day darker. 'The girl gets all, does she? Well, I
shall retain my interest in her though it be from a distance! You
may sit in your grand house, sweetheart, but one day I'll come
calling again!'

He swung himself to the saddle again, cut the horse with a
savage blow of his whip and cantered away.

I sat motionless, staring after him.

'That was your father,' Mr Brunty said, coming to sit beside
me again. 'That was Mr Heathcliff.'

TWO

I pause here, looking at that first entry, those plain unadorned words. Grandfather died. My father came.

My father that sneering stranger on the black horse? I didn't want to believe it any more than I wanted to believe that dark being had sired me. Yet I felt curiosity growing as the months following my grandfather's funeral passed and the house sank into a damp winter.

Outwardly nothing much altered. Grandfather lay in the church between his wife and daughter, and Mr Alistair took over the affairs of the estate, arriving twice a week to sit in my grandfather's study and go over the books and the rent rolls. Brigit had always seen to the buying in of food as well as the caring for me and that simply continued and as my grandfather was no longer alive to teach me my letters a tutor came three times a week to school me. It was almost as if my father had never visited.

In this fashion three years passed, proved to me by the next entry in my journal.

'Mr Hugh Brunty told me of my father.'

And the whole day leaps into my mind as if it happened only last week. It was summer-time, a month or two before my twelfth birthday and the glens and fields were lustrous with sunbeams that turned the spiders' webs in the long grass into twinkling nets of gold. I had no lessons during the summer and as Brigit also took a few days to visit her relatives who lived further south I was thrown upon my own devices, which pleased me as I liked to imagine that I was mistress of the whole house.

I was not, however, inclined to stay within doors. So I took long rides on Jackdaw, packing a saddle-bag with food for the day and liking to explore the hidden places that lay beyond the farms and the houses and the village green.

On this day I had ridden out towards Imdel Fort, passing the half-acre of ripe corn with the stone bothy at one end. A track led past the latter to the fort itself with its ruined tower and the wild flowers thrusting their way through the tumbled stones. I saw Mr Brunty scything the cornstalks and his eldest son, Patrick, gleaning in his wake and I took off my wide-brimmed hat and waved to them with it as I cantered past.

Even on sunny afternoons the old fort had a sinister aspect, its half derelict interior filled with shadows cast, I knew, by the tall thin trees that ringed it round but assuming goblin shapes if one shut one's eyes and opened one's mind and let the images flood in.

I dismounted and left Jackdaw to graze among the fallen rocks and the springing flowers and left my luncheon in its bag at one side for the scents around me satisfied my appetite for a while.

Then I heard boots crunching on the stony track and Mr Brunty came into view, his scythe over his shoulder, with his taller son following after.

'Good day to you, Miss Aspen.'

He laid down his scythe and took a seat near me on a lump of rock that had been moulded by wind and weather into a stool.

'Good day, Mr Brunty. Good day, Patrick,' I answered.

Patrick who was sixteen and obviously despised twelve-year-olds nodded and folded his long legs under him as he too sank to the ground.

He was not only tall but thin as if he had partly outgrown his strength and must fight to regain it. He had the pale skin of the Bruntys with the eyes of his mother painted in a paler blue and his father's hair darkened from sandy to auburn.

'Brigit still off visiting?' Mr Brunty enquired.

I nodded, putting a question of my own, 'How are the twins?'

Ellis Brunty had kept her word, waiting three years before she brought another child into the world and then presenting her husband with two girls at once.

'Both thriving!' he replied happily. 'They're to be Rose and Sarah – pretty names I think.'

'Very pretty,' I agreed.

'And why are you up at this old fort all by yourself?' he enquired genially. 'You don't find it lonely?'

'I like lonely places sometimes,' I confided. 'At the house there is Brigit bustling about and the other servants forever dusting the only room you feel like sitting down in, and then Mr Alistair comes to do the accounts and Mr Brewster to tutor me.'

'Sounds like a hint for us to leave, Pat,' Mr Brunty said, winking at his son.

'Oh, I don't mind friends,' I said hastily, 'if they have something interesting to tell.'

'Like?' His steady grey eyes fixed themselves on my face.

'About real people,' I told him. 'About my father.'

'He's not been back?' he said somewhat sharply.

'No, but I still remember him,' I said. 'He came and grandfather died. Since then I've heard nothing from him or of him.'

'And you want to know?'

I nodded again. 'People need to know where they came from,' I said.

'Aye, that's true. My own history bears that out,' he said. 'I was taken from my parents when I was seven years old. An uncle and aunt arrived at our farm just after my father died. My mother had four younger than myself and found it hard to manage but Uncle Welsh, that was his name, gave her fifty pounds and they took me on a long journey north of the Boyne to another farm where my uncle treated me very badly, made me sleep in the stable and do heavy work about the farm. When I tried to run away he would thrash me and many a night I sobbed myself to sleep on rough hay.'

'But you did get away,' I prompted.

'Not for eleven years,' he told me. 'My uncle had no family feeling for me because he himself had been taken into our clan as a foundling by my grandfather, and his wife, Mary, was my blood aunt though she never dared remind him of it. I had a friend though. I had a dog, a stray mongrel, that attached itself to me and followed where I went. I named him Keeper and it was a grief to me that when at last I fled over the river I had to leave him behind for he was old and lame by then.'

'You went home?' I questioned.

'The old place had been abandoned.' A look of remembered pain flitted over his face. 'Nobody could tell me what had happened. The house was empty with the chimney-stack fallen and the doors hanging on their hinges and the land was over-grown with tares and roots. I think that perhaps my mother and the younger ones took ship for the Americas but I have never found the truth of it.'

'And then?'

'I found work in the lime kilns. It was hard work and poorly paid and yet it was better than I had known before. But Paddy McClory lived just over the border and he befriended me, brought food, found some clothes to hide my rags.'

'And you married his sister,' I said.

'Aye, Ellis came by one day,' he said, and the look in his eyes

26

told me he lived the scene again. 'I'd fallen the day before and cut my face on a boulder and she had heard of it and ridden to see what she could do. She was just sixteen years old and I'd heard of her beauty, but it was greater than the tales told of it for she had hair like golden threads and blue, blue eyes and she knelt before me and wiped the dried blood away and smeared ointment on the scratches and chafed my bruised hands and spoke to me in the old tongue like the rippling of a stream in midsummer. And I loved her from that instant. She came many times and it was weeks before I dared hope that more than pity moved her but one day she said to me, very low and sweet, "I think you and I share a soul, Hugh. I feel it in my heart." I didn't answer for a long time and then I said, roughly, to test hers, "Like *Beauty and the Beast* I daresay, with me to set against your loveliness like black against white!"

'And she took my face between her long fingers and said, "But the Beast was always a handsome prince and Beauty loved him from the beginning and went on loving him past the ending of time. Don't you know that, my dear? Don't you know?"

'And then I did know and nothing has separated us since. She is twined in my roots like a silver thread and always will be.'

He finished and fell silent with a smile on his lips. The deepening sunlight had burnished his hair to gold and his eyes were full of memories and I wished that I had not suddenly known at that moment, without knowing how I knew, that he would not live to beget grey hairs and that his heart's desire would remain long years above ground while he slept in the peaty earth.

'That,' said Patrick, 'is a beautiful tale.'

'And a true one.' Mr Brunty laughed and ruffled my hair. 'Our Pat likes a good tale especially if it be true, don't you, son? You know he has it in mind to open a school for the younglings hereabouts! Now there is ambition for you, eh?'

'A body never got on without ambition,' Patrick said in a tone

27

of haughty indifference but he laid his hand upon his father's shoulder and pressed it gently, affectionately.

'And we must be away home!' Mr Brunty said, rising and picking up his scythe. 'We've the stocks to bind and the gleanings to gather before rain arrives. And you'd best be off home yourself, Miss Aspen, or the maidservants will be rushing all over Ireland trying to find you!'

'But you've not told me about my father!' I protested.

He looked at me gravely for a moment, then turning to his son said, 'Pat, run home and tell your mother that I'll not be long. Miss Aspen wants the story she asked for at the beginning.'

'Mother will have supper ready,' Patrick said with a darkling look in my direction. 'She'll not be happy to serve you cold taters because you stayed talking to a child.'

I lowered my eyes and said nothing but I resolved in that moment that Patrick Brunty would pay one day for being so contemptuous of my need.

'I'll not be long,' Hugh Brunty said, and Patrick took up the scythe and went down the track with it.

'It's hard for him,' his father said, 'to be always sharing the love with all the younger ones. Now, my honey, wrap your cloak about you for though my tale's short it may chill your bones even on a summer's day.'

I did as he bade and listened as he told his tale, his voice low and strained as if the matter of it troubled him.

'Thirteen years back in the summer of 'eighty I went to Dublin on a matter of business for Mr Stewart. Ellis and I lived then in the old bothy down there for we'd not built the bigger dwelling which was needed when the family increased. Pat was three years old and William was one and Ellis was in the family way again, so the extra money from Mr Stewart came in useful. You've never been to Dublin else you'd know it's a crowded port with vessels from all over the world arriving there and a dozen different tongues spoken and a hundred different crimes committed every waking day. I took a room at an inn and was fortunate not to have to share though the room was small and not overclean, but I finished my business and made a good supper and then went for a stroll along the quay. There were taverns in plenty but I was never a drinking man so I just wandered along and listened to the folk talking and shouting all around me.'

'And you met my father,' I prompted.

'I met a lad,' Mr Brunty said. 'Not older than seventeen with the fuzz still sparse on his face and long black hair matted to his shoulders and the look of a wild animal trapped in a desert of vultures. He was crouching against a bale of sacks and God knows why I stopped but something about him reminded me of myself. Anyway, I held out my hand and he took it and walked with me to the inn, I say walked but he limped rather for the soles of his shoes were worn through. At the inn I paid for him to have a bath and then I bought him a good supper. He said nothing until I made up a bed for myself on the floor and bade him take my bed and then he raised himself on one elbow and stared at me with those black, brooding eyes and said at last, 'My name is Heathcliff. Thank you.'

And then he lay down and slept though three times in his sleep I heard him mutter something.'

'What?'

'It sounded like Cathy. I didn't wake him nor ask him later. In the morning I prised out of him the fact that his name was Heathcliff only and that he had neither parents nor home. He knew how to read and write he said and was skilled in farm work. He wasn't Irish but there was a look of the gypsy about him. I suspected he'd stowed away on a ship at Liverpool or Manchester but he never said. Before we left Dublin I spent more money on decent boots and trousers and jacket for him and we took turns to ride the horse. I'd no work to offer him but Mr Stewart was a kindly man and he offered him a place. I saw him now and then when I'd occasion to visit your grandfather's but he hardly lifted his head from his task to nod to me and I heard from the other farmhands that he was sullen and silent always.

But Mr Stewart took a liking to him and would let him into the study to borrow books and Miss Rosina used to help him with the words that he found difficult to read.'

'My mother helped him?'

'Aye. Miss Rosina was not more than sixteen herself but she was well read and patient and sweet. I saw them now and then, she on her pony with a book in one hand while he walked by her side, holding the reins, listening to her as she read aloud. It made me uneasy because once or twice he glanced up as I passed and there was mockery in his black eyes as if he secretly made game of her kindliness.'

'And then?'

'One day I heard that they had been wed,' he said slowly and reluctantly. 'They were wed in Dublin it was said with only Mr Stewart to give his daughter away. There was gossip about it because our brides have their weddings here usually, unless they run away together as my Ellis and I did.'

'So grandfather approved,' I said.

'Maybe he'd no option,' Hugh Brunty said with a certain grimness. 'Mr Heathcliff, as he began to style himself, went to live in the big house and Mr Stewart entrusted him with business, for your grandfather had many interests beyond farming, so Mr Heathcliff was often absent for long periods. Then you were born.'

'How long after the——?'

'Oh, several months. I have no head for dates,' he answered somewhat hastily.

'And my mother died,' I said sadly.

'Aye.' He put his arm about my shoulders and held me so for a moment or two before he released me. 'She died a few hours after you arrived in this world. Mr Heathcliff was due home from a business trip and when he came and saw the drawn curtains and heard the keening he went up the steps and through the front door and a hush fell among those good people as if something malign had landed in their midst. Then he said, "So I am a widower?"

And laughed. Laughed, Miss Aspen, as though something amused him. And then he went over to Brigit who held you in her arms and took you from her and looked down at you and laughed again, saying, "By God, she has a look of me about her! Her name shall be Aspen."

"Aspen Stewart," your grandfather said fiercely.

"As you please," said Mr Heathcliff, "for there's little in a name. I shall work for you for another year and a day and then you may keep the babe here if you wish for I shall be going on a long journey and may not return, but if I ever do you will remember the girl Aspen is flesh of my flesh and blood of my blood and bone of my bone as much as that frail thing that lies there."

And he gave you into Brigit's arms again and walked out. He never attended the funeral nor wore any mourning band but he kept his word; did the work for which he was most handsomely paid; took long trips in pursuit of that business whatever it was; was seen now and then about the house and, a year and a day after the wake left and never returned until the day your grandfather, God rest his soul, went to his Maker.'

'Mr Brunty,' I asked abruptly, 'how did grandfather die?'

'A sudden heart attack,' he replied. 'Mr Heathcliff was with him in the study and then Mr Heathcliff came out and told Brigit her master was ailing, and to be sure the old gentleman's health was not too hearty. He came next on the day of the wake, angry because he had learned that your grandfather's will left all to you. But you saw him then.'

'Yes,' I said, my thoughts jumbling in my head. There were more queries on the tip of my tongue but Mr Brunty bestirred himself, going to untie my pony's halter and lifting me to his back.

'Best forget your father,' he said brusquely. 'He's a man more welcome in his absence than his coming.'

And yet I knew even then that the whole tale had not been told, though perhaps Hugh Brunty had related most of what he knew.

He walked with me as far as the gates and left me there, waving after me as I rode up the drive.

That night I couldn't sleep. Brigit was still away and as there was no risk of her stealing in to ensure I hadn't thrown off the bedcovers as she still sometimes did as if I had been a small girl, I rose when the clock struck two and put on my dressing-gown and sat by the window, looking out through the gap in the curtains until drowsiness claimed me again and I went back to my bed.

The day wears on, shorter here than in the south, night hurrying in to shroud the houses. I have been sitting still too long and my limbs crave exercise. Tomorrow I will hire a horse but this evening I will walk for a while. Long walks were always my pleasure at home.

I shut the journal and put on my cloak and boots and step out of the bedchamber into a short passage that brings me to the head of the stairs. The staircase leads down into the main taproom where a number of gentlemen – more yokel than gentleman some of them – are gathered.

One of them, a gentleman from his dress and manner, rises from his chair to allow me to pass him. He bows slightly as he does so but his mind is not on young ladies. He holds a fan of cards in his hand and I hear one of the others seated at that table say, 'Do you bid high or low, Mr Lockwood?'

'Low. Dame Fortune is not with me these days,' he answers, somewhat moodily I think, and resumes his seat again.

I open the door of the inn and stand for a moment looking out into the evening. To the right the main street plunges down past houses from whose windows gleams of light issue. To the left I can see the outline of steps mounting at an angle to a dark church, walled in stone and, within the walls, stones laid flat and others standing askew in a graveyard that extends further than I can see.

The street is not silent. People are walking up the hill as if it were level; others lean against half-open doors and gossip in the thick northern dialect which I find so hard to follow.

I turn to the left and see a lane that runs up sharply past the church. There is a lantern flaring from a pole to guide one's footsteps and I feel the breeze, warmer than I expected, on my face.

The lane itself widens and I reach an iron gate set into the wall. For a moment I pause, looking through the bars, seeing beyond the gate a patch of turf and a house set sideways on at the other side of a weedy path, the outlines of the building illuminated by a lamp held by someone who stands on the step, door half open behind her, and calls out in a tone edged with amused irritation, 'Keeper! Here, boy! This minute or you will spend the night in the yard!'

I would have thought the tall, thin figure to be that of a lad but it wears a long dark dress and clutches a shawl above a small, high bosom. She shields the lantern with her hand and I glimpse long, tapering fingers painted red by the flame within the glass. Then I walk on, aware that I am on the verge of trespassing and pass outhouses and on the other side two buildings joined by a mutual wall, and stand at last on a dirt path with a stile a few yards ahead and fields beyond that, with just visible below the horizon, a sweep of scrubland and grass.

There is something harsh and bitter in the land here, something that lurks beneath the surface like an animal held in check by a leash that, if broken, will free it to spring and attack. It calls to something within me, something at which Brigit has never guessed.

Somewhere I hear laughter and the sound of voices and I turn and go back down the lane, past the iron gate in the high wall. My eyes stray in that direction but the figure has gone and the house is dark and inviolate again.

In the morning I will explore further. Meanwhile I make my way the short distance to the inn and enter the warmth and the brightness again.

'Is everything all right, Miss Stewart?'

The buxom woman serving behind the bar comes forward to greet me.

'Perfectly,' I tell her. 'I went out for a breath of night air, that's all.'

And I pass the card-playing gentlemen and go up the stairs to my bedchamber again, still feeling the need for exercise but more weary than I realized before.

My journal lies on the table still, mutely inviting me to open it. I hang up my cloak, pull off my boots and stir up the coals in the fireplace into a blaze. Now I sit here, pen in hand, seeing my own writing like sooty marks on the white page.

'Tell me about my father,' I demanded of Brigit when she was home again after visiting her relatives.

She threw me a startled look and shook her head.

'I know something of him,' I persisted. 'Mr Brunty told me—'

'Hugh Brunty had best keep his information to himself, Miss Aspen!' she answered sharply. 'Mr Stewart, God rest his soul, would not have wanted his name mentioned in this house.'

'But he stayed on here for a year and a day after I was born and my mother died,' I argued. 'Why did it not happen that my grandfather turned him out of doors if he hated him so much?'

'They had business affairs to settle,' she said briefly.

'What business?' I persisted. 'Mr Heathcliff went away for long periods during that time. Mr Alistair deals with the horse-breeding sales and the land rentals. Why did my fath—?'

'That's quite enough, Miss Aspen!' she interrupted. 'Your late, dear grandfather, God rest his soul, made it plain that your father, when he came here, was to speak only with him, and when he finally left we were warned not to mention him again.'

'Did he treat my mother badly?' I persisted. 'Did he marry her for her money? I've read tales—'

'Ruining your eyesight with tales not meant for younglings!' she said crossly. 'Yes, partly for money, I suppose, for Mr Stewart was a warm man with many business dealings, but not only for that. I don't know the whole of it and you're too young to hear any of it.'

'I will be twelve very soon,' I said haughtily.

'Not for two months so you may stop your fretting and sit down to your tea like a good girl!'

'Do you think he will visit us again?' I enquired.

'Mother of God! I hope not,' she said, not loudly but quietly as if she feared he might hear her and stride up to the front steps.

'He was very handsome,' I said.

'He was that!' She coloured slightly as she spoke, as if his dark beauty had touched even her stout soul. 'That's the snare the devil uses, Miss Aspen. Talk of something else, do.'

I have blotted the page and laid my pen aside. The bed here is comfortable as I ease myself into the pillows, white linen under black tresses tinged with red. My eyelids feel heavy and beyond the window the lights from the houses opposite are flickering out and the sounds from the bar below are muted and indistinct.

Tomorrow I will call at the house I passed and make some excuse to enter it. I want to know why two dogs should have the same name – not a name one usually bestows upon a dog.

Drifting into sleep I can hear inside my head that amused voice with its edge of irritation calling for Keeper to return. But the voice grows fainter as if a wind were bearing it away over the wastes of the moor beyond the lane and the fields. What I hear now, faint but clear, in some place outside myself where part of myself resides, is a lad's voice, broken into fragments by long, sobbing breaths, the word Cathy splintering into slivers against the dingy walls of a Dublin hostelry.

THREE

This morning I rose, washed and dressed myself. I wore one of my plainest frocks since I have no wish to attract overmuch attention in the village. When I arrive I want the surprise to be total.

I breakfasted in the snug behind the bar. The gentleman who made room for me last night was there, drinking his coffee at the next table, newspaper folded beside his plate. He rose as I entered and made a polite bow. Then he resumed his seat and read his newspaper, leaving me to partake of the simple repast I had stipulated. Now and then he glanced in my direction but his shyness was obviously greater than his interest and, for my own part, I have no desire to pursue what must be a brief acquaintance.

After breakfast I resolved to take a walk. Before I present myself I want to get to know the surrounding landscape a little better, and I had thoughts of taking a closer look at the house in the lane.

The morning was mellow when I left the inn though now as I sit before my journal the sky outside is lowering, threatening rain.

Certainly it is a noisy village! As soon as I stepped outdoors my ears were assailed by clattering of clogs down the main street, by the monotonous chipping of axe against stone some-where in the bleak graveyard, by a group of women clustered about a shop window and talking of something or other in accents so broad that I could hardly distinguish one word from its neighbours.

I turned up the lane and walked to the iron gates. In daylight the small garden looked more unkempt, robbed as it was of night's enchantment, and the house looked small and unim-pressive.

A man in clerical garb was issuing from the front door as I paused and gave me a glance of enquiry as I stood aside to allow him to open the gate.

'Good morning. May I help you?' he said diffidently.

'Are you the vicar here?' I enquired.

'We are not yet a separate parish so my position is that of curate,' he said. 'I am James Charnock, Miss—?'

'Stewart,' I said, taking the offered hand and shaking it. The name evidently meant nothing to him.

I went on, not really wishing to detain him, 'I merely wondered if Keeper got home last night.'

'I beg your pardon?'

'Keeper. I assumed Keeper was a dog when I heard the young lady calling him.'

'From here?' he said, frowning slightly.

'She stood on the front steps with a lamp in her hand,' I said, turning to indicate the spot. 'She was calling for Keeper and as I know of another dog with that name—'

'Miss er – Stewart, I live alone,' he said, the sudden frost in his tone threatening to mar the mellowness of the morning. 'No lady, young or otherwise, lives at this dwelling. You must've been mistaken. Good morning to you.'

He raised his hat and went down the lane towards the church. I stared at the house a moment more and then, seeking to dismiss the matter from my mind, I walked on to where the stile both barred and gave access to the fields and the moors beyond.

They were golden brown under the then clear sky, rising and falling with here and there a patch of black as if someone had spilt ink on a pretty dress, and dotted here and there great swathes of gorse. I could discern one or two dwellings further along, low walls enclosing them and holly bushes, ripening from green to red with pale veined leaves nearer to where I stood.

Then I felt a cold draught of air stir my skirt and the hem of my cloak and high above me a skein of wild geese with necks outstretched flew southward in perfect formation.

Now the sky outside the window harbours rain and the lamps are lit in my bedchamber though it is scarcely afternoon. It occurs to me as I flip open the pages of my journal that I made curious use of that white paper. I wrote nothing of the seasons, of the years when I suffered from any trifling ailment, of the strange dreams that visited me when my child's frame began to develop into that of a young woman, curves and hollows marking the speeding years while my mind remained alert and aware, puzzling over half-answered questions and Brigit dwindling into middle age as the babe she had nurtured grew beyond the control of her caring.

The third entry in all that virgin space read like an echo. 'My father came again.'

It seems to me that my life is hinged on those rare events, like signposts in a wilderness.

I had reached the age of fifteen a week before and felt myself to be almost my own mistress. Mr Brewster had ceased his lessons with me a twelvemonth previously. He had applied for and been offered a post at a boys' school in Cork and had left the district. I was not sorry to see him leave though he had been a pleasant teacher but I wanted to learn more than lay in books.

Mr Alistair, at the house to do the accounting, failed to agree.

'Perhaps we should think of a governess for the ladylike arts?' he suggested.

'Playing the pianoforte and dancing the quadrille?' I said. 'I am not interested in petty amusements, sir! I already know how to sew and paint a flower in a vase. I wish to learn more about the estate and the running of it so that I may the better understand when you quote prices and profits at me.'

'When you are of age all that will be made manifest to you,' he answered.

His speaking always had a tinge of pomposity about it.

'We shall see,' I answered sweetly.

'Meanwhile if you wish to learn something more suited to your future state,' he said, biting the end of his little finger thoughtfully, 'you might consider more advanced literature, or-or a language – many young ladies are entering upon the study of French, even Latin. Now Master Brunty has, I know, studied Latin in his own time and—'

'Pat Brunty,' I broke in, 'keeps a village school in a shed he rents for six days labour a year!'

'Very neatly transformed into a schoolroom,' Mr Alistair said. 'And he is proving himself a born teacher though to be sure his pupils have no need of Latin! But he is ambitious, Miss Aspen, and were you to attend some of his lessons his reputation would not suffer!'

I hid a smile at his notion of me as a Lady Bountiful, a patron of the worthy poor, and the image of Hugh Brunty's eldest son flashed into my mind. He was eighteen or nineteen now, still tall and spare with that dark red hair and pale eyes and long tapering fingers. Handsome, some might have said, but with the arrogant bearing of a youth determined to better his betters. He was, in his own eyes at least, the pride of the herd which now numbered ten, Alice having just been born, a miniature edition of her still beautiful mother.

'I will think about it,' I said.

That happened six months ago and I still smile inwardly when I remember the swift consequences.

On my fifteenth birthday I gave orders that I wished not to be disturbed. Brigit, grumbling, took herself off somewhere and I was free to amuse myself as I wished. Accordingly I went into the study, unlocked the desk and abstracted the rent rolls and other documents pertaining to the management of the estate. I had, I assumed, the right to find out if I was being cheated or deceived in any manner though to be plain I did not regard Mr Alistair as a dishonest man.

Everything, as I had expected, looked to be in order. I went through the rent rolls, the profit and loss columns for livestock and crops, the wages paid to the servants. There were the payments to Mr Brewster and to Mr Alistair, receipted bills for food and other necessities arranged in order. There was a copy of grandfather's will, that I had not yet seen, leaving everything to 'my beloved granddaughter' naming Mr Alistair as trustee until I attained my majority. There were payments to my father, increasingly large payments I noted, details of some business that seemed to have been transacted in the Far East. My father had signed these in a sharp, angular hand but the last one was dated just after my first birthday and there were no more after that.

I locked everything away again and sat for a spell with my chin in my hands, brooding. Whatever had been between grandfather and my father had made the latter rich.

After a while I rose and ordered that Jackdaw be saddled. The pony was elderly now and slower than she had been and even Brigit had stopped fussing over the possibility that I might break my neck when I rode out alone.

I think that something in me knew that he would come. I felt him in my bones. I rode up to the old fort where the stones made sinister shapes against the sky and he was already there, his horse grazing near at hand and he seated on the stool-fashioned rock where Hugh Brunty had told me the twin tales of himself and Mr Heathcliff.

'You were fifteen a few days ago,' he remarked without greeting.

'I was,' I said. 'Have you brought me a present?'

'No.'

He spoke lazily, leaning back slightly, his black eyes unwavering as he watched me seat myself on an adjoining rock.

'I expected none,' I said briefly.

'Not even from a sweetheart?'

'I have no sweetheart,' I said. 'I am too young.'

'Intent upon your books I daresay,' he said with a slight curling of his lip, which might have been interpreted as a smile.

'You have heard gossip?' I felt my face redden.

'I've not been in Ireland these three years,' he said. 'So you do have something to tell me?'

'Hugh Brunty's eldest son, Patrick—' I began.

'I remember Hugh Brunty. You've not been snuggling up to an Irish peasant, for God's sake!'

'His son,' I said, 'is ambitious and arrogant. He never liked me.'

'You expect the whole world to love you?' He gave a short bark of laughter. 'Then you're a fool and no offspring of mine!'

'I don't expect a peasant boy to look down on me because he sees me as a child!' I said angrily.

'Did he so? And what revenge did you take?'

'Pat Brunty started a school,' I said, 'for the village children. My tutor left and I went to his school—'

'To learn with peasants?'

'For private tuition. Pat has taught himself Latin and he is a good teacher. People round here speak highly of him still.'

'Still?' He folded his arms and stared at me.

'I went for a three month period,' I said. 'Twice a week. We sat in the shed he rents and he taught me Latin. He was pleased that I am intelligent with a good memory. Sometimes he was only a page or two ahead of me. The weather was fine and sometimes he would lock up the place and we would walk, declaiming verbs as we went. And he began to look at me as young men look at girls.'

'Did he so?' he said without expression.

'I smiled back at him,' I said. 'Once as we walked he put his arm about my shoulders and one of the village women passed us. As she did so I broke away from his grasp, frowning, hurrying ahead as if his touch displeased me. I saw her staring and I laughed inside myself at her and at Pat Brunty with his Latin and his talk of rising in the world.'

'And then?' His voice was soft as a caress.

'After a few weeks I went to Mr Alistair and told him that Pat Brunty was more interested in making advances to me than in grounding me in Latin. Mr Alistair agreed that such a teacher was not worthy of his place and that I should leave off my lessons. The village woman talked as I knew she would and the rumours multiplied and very soon that old shed that Pat Brunty considered his pride and joy was shut down and he found another post further north. I will not be looked down upon by anyone!'

'Will you not?' my father said. There was approval in his voice and then he sprang up with the litheness of a tiger and caught me a blow across the face that sent me reeling.

I cried out in pain and outrage and swayed for an instant longer before a red mist came over me and I launched myself at him, kicking at his shins, twisting my head to bite the long iron fingers that held me. And in the midst of the redness that turned the air to blood I heard his laughter as he pulled me towards him, kissed me hard upon the mouth and let me go so abruptly that I sat down heavily on a rock and shook my head to clear it of the whirling confusion.

'The slap,' he said, resuming his position, 'was to teach you not to flirt with upstart peasants and the kiss was to remind you that you are more than a match for any upstart. By God, but I hope my son shows the same brave spirit!'

'You have a son too?'

'Twelve years old, born in the same month as yourself.'

'What is his name? Did you marry again?'

'I mind enough about respectability not to strew bastards about the world,' he said. 'I wed again nearly thirteen years since. My wife ran away within two months of our mating and lives in London now. I have never laid eyes on Linton but if he is like his fool of a mother he'll be no source of pride to me. However I've plans for him and when his mother dies I shall have him home with me.'

'Home being. . . ?'

'None of your affair,' he said brusquely.

'So you have loved two women?' I said.

'I have loved one and she was never my wife,' he said and I saw the muscles in his jaw clench though whether in anger or anguish was impossible to tell.

'You didn't love my mother?'

It was a stupid, infantile question. I knew it even as I put it.

'Rosina Stewart served my purpose,' he said. 'She was a pretty thing and there was a kindness in her that might have borne fruit with a different husband. I was not glad when she died for my hope of a true marriage was gone but neither did I grieve. And she left a daughter for whom I have plans – not settled yet but seething in my brain. Now go home before I forget we are close kin and kiss you again!'

He strode to his horse and mounted up and as he spurred away I saw again in a flash of sunlight what I had seen once before and almost forgotten: the woman made of air hard behind him on the saddle though even as I glimpsed her shape it drifted like tiny fallen clouds into the blue air around and then was visible no more.

I felt cold despite the sun as I mounted Jackdaw and took the stony track past the old bothy towards my home. That my father would come again I felt sure but only the devil would know when.

As I jogged home I took it into my head to visit Ellis Brunty again. I had not yet seen the latest arrival which was remiss of me; indeed I had seen very little of the Bruntys since their son had his school closed down and himself gone off to tutor somewhere or other.

I saw the others, of course, but always, it seemed to me, at a distance. Even the little girls hastened out of my way if they chanced to see me passing, hurrying within doors, and though Mr Brunty nodded if we passed he didn't stop and talk as he once would have done. No doubt they believed Pat's version of events but, though I had quite deliberately encouraged him, it seemed to me that he had needed little urging on my part.

Now I rode along towards the Brunty house, seeing caps raised as I passed other cottages. One or two raised their hands in greeting but the days when people used to stop me to talk for a few minutes seemed to have vanished along with my childhood. Or perhaps some of them remembered my father's coming into the neighbourhood.

William, the second Brunty son, was slouching along the street, hands deep in his pockets and head bent as he moodily kicked stones ahead of him. At seventeen he had not yet settled into any regular occupation but took on odd labouring jobs, even competed at fairs in boxing, Brigit said.

'Always ready to fight somebody,' she had mentioned recently. 'Drinks more than he should they say too.'

No doubt gossip had filled out the juicier details where William Brunty was concerned but he scarcely raised his eyes as I trotted past. His younger brothers, the tall Hugh and the stocky James, were sat on the garden wall, swinging their legs and whispering together.

'Mam's in,' the latter announced as I dismounted and tied Jackdaw to the gatepost.

'I have some things for the babby in my saddle-bag,' I told him.

Indeed they had been there for some days waiting for me to find an opportunity to visit.

I went up the short path and tapped at the door. Seven-year-old Jane opened it and backed into the room behind, saying over her shoulder, 'Mam, Miss Aspen's come!'

'Peace be on this house,' I said in the traditional mode of greeting as I went over to the hearth, laid but not lit with peat and twigs and dried pine-cones.

Ellis sat in the rocking chair, her feet on the hearthstone, the baby at her breast.

'Don't get up!' I said hastily. 'I wanted to bring these I sewed for the baby's coming. Are you well?'

'Quite well, Miss Aspen.' Her face was as serenely lovely as ever but I sensed a slight withdrawal in her manner. 'I'm a mite fretted about my Hugh though. He works too hard and he's a cough on him that'd irritate the angels!'

'I can have something sent down to you for that,' I said.

A slight tinge flushed her cheeks.

'Thank you kindly, Miss Aspen,' she said, 'but we can tend our own down in the village.'

She hadn't asked me to sit down but I did so anyway, folding my hands in my lap and hesitating before I blurted out, 'Mrs

Brunty, I'm very sorry about . . . how is your son?'

'Oh, Pat would never have been happy with just a village school,' she said, her manner thawing slightly. 'He is very suited in his present post and he's saving his money carefully. One day he hopes to leave Ireland and enter one of the professions in England – the Army perhaps, for he's a good shot for all that his sight is slightly weak, or he might become a poet though there do always seem to be a mighty number of poets about!'

'It wasn't really his fault,' I began awkwardly.

'No good crying for milk when the cow's kicked the pail over,' she said with a slight smile. 'Pat's well enough where he is. It's our William I worry about, rushing off to meetings about a united Ireland and not settling to anything steady. My Hugh says he was just the same at that age but he'd more reason to be after the manner in which his uncle treated him!'

'My father was about seventeen when he came here, wasn't he?' I said.

'Yes. Yes, he was.'

'I saw him again today.'

'There was talk he'd been seen in the neighbourhood,' she said.

'Mrs Brunty, what was my mother like?' I asked. 'What was Rosina Stewart like?'

'We were much the same age as I recall,' she said slowly, shifting Alice to her other breast. 'I lived on the McClory farm with my brothers and she lived at the big house. Old Mrs Stewart died when Rosina was just a babe and so Mr Stewart always took close care of his daughter. We met at church now and then for your grandfather was friendly with our priest and sometimes they'd attend a mass. She was small and her hair was red, more a strawberry red than anything else, and she was always very prettily clad, but she was always either with her father or one of the servants.'

'And she fell in love with Mr Heathcliff,' I prompted.

'Well, he wasn't exactly Mr Heathcliff then,' she demurred. 'He was just a lad fallen on hard times to whom your grandfather took a liking. Much rougher than he became after your grandfather took him into his personal service. Your mother helped him with his reading and writing one of the servants told me.'

'And they married.' I fixed my eyes upon her and said, 'How long after they married was I born?'

'Miss Aspen, those are not things to be talked about in front of children!'

She nodded towards Jane who was playing with a humming top. 'Then you need not say,' I said, nodding at her to establish the fact that I was fifteen and not entirely ignorant.

'Why these questions, Miss Aspen?' she enquired softly.

'I hoped there might have been love,' I said.

'I believe your father was not . . . unkind to her,' she said after a little pause.

'But it was not like you and Mr Brunty?'

'Love can nourish or destroy,' she said slowly. 'For Hugh and me, it nourishes us both and the children we have. Others may warm their hands at our flame. When you meet a man, Miss Aspen, seek that kind of loving between you both. Not the kind that destroys what it feeds on. I tell you if one of us was to die the other would carry on because that's life's way, though I love the very bones of him!'

She paused to lift Alice to her shoulder as the door opened and Hugh Brunty came in.

'The lads said Miss Aspen was here,' he said. 'It's kind of you to visit, Miss Aspen.'

'She brought some pretty things for Alice,' Ellis Brunty said.

'I ought to have come before,' I said awkwardly.

'I'll walk home with you part way,' he said. 'Or would you be staying for a bite of supper now?'

I wanted to remain longer in that warm bright room with the sun streaming through the casement and the fire laid ready for the evening but having made a sort of peace I thought it wiser to go.

'Jackdaw looks a mite lame,' he observed when we were outside.

'Surely not! I didn't ride her far!' I protested.

'Well, she's an old girl,' he granted. 'We'll walk for a spell and see how she fares. The baby's a beauty, isn't she?'

'A real beauty!' I agreed.

'And you saw your father.'

'You saw him too?'

We were walking along the village street and I looked at him.

'For a few seconds only. I hoped we'd seen the last of him but he arrives like an ill wind from time to time,' he said.

'You were the one brought him here in the beginning,' I said almost accusingly.

'Aye, that's so. Perhaps he'd've found his way here anyway. Who knows? Anyway he came and—'

'Married my mother,' I broke in. 'Did my grandfather pay him to wed her? Was that the way of it?'

'I wasn't privy to their arrangements. Miss Aspen, why don't you put this out of your head? You've seen your father less than half a dozen times in all your life. It's possible he won't come here again.'

'You know that he will,' I said.

'You own a handsome estate, Miss Aspen.' He took Jackdaw's rein as we turned off towards the main gates of my property. 'I know your grandfather paid him handsomely for the work he did for him, and I know that Mr Alistair isn't a man to be bribed or to be cheated. Your inheritance is safe.'

'My father comes to see me,' I said stiffly.

'Aye, maybe so, but he also ferrets about the Stewart farm,' my companion said. 'And I'd wager he knows to the last penny the value of every acre and every bushel of corn.'

'He wasn't unkind to my mother.'

'He wasn't here often enough! Always off to Dublin, to Bristol, to Lord knows where, making the deals for your grandfather – and don't ask me what they were for I've no idea!'

'And my mother loved him.'

'She did for he'd a way with women, purred like a cat when he found it to his advantage. After they wed Miss Rosina lost her sparkle, grew quiet and melancholy like. When he went away she stayed indoors most of the time. When he was home she seemed on edge, like someone fearful of starting an eruption but I never heard he misused her.'

'I see,' I said slowly.

We had reached the gates and I took the rein from him and said, 'Mr Brunty, when Jackdaw really sickens will you come and make a peaceful end for her?'

'I will, Miss Aspen. She's a way to go yet though before you need to summon me,' he said.

'Your son . . .' I began.

'Pat will make his own way in the world,' he told me and bent suddenly in a spasm of coughing.

'Mr Brunty?'

'A touch of the ague, Miss Aspen. At forty a man must expect a few aches and pains. Don't you be worrying about Pat now!'

He pressed my hand and walked off down the track and I saw the sun glinting on his hair, turning it from sandy to gold.

FOUR

To sit here, I decided this morning, is foolish. What does it gain me to read the brief entries in my journal and let my memories clothe them with substance? He told me to travel here and I obeyed.

The pleasant-looking young gentleman whom they addressed as Mr Lockwood has left, climbing up into a coach with a distinct air of relief. I could leave too if I wished. Nobody has marked my coming nor will question my going. Once only did the landlady, bringing me fresh coffee, look at me with sudden attention as if she recognized something in the tilt of my head or the darkness of my eyes but she instantly looked away again as if she shrugged off an unwelcome thought.

I shut my journal and put on my boots and went out down the lane past the house where the curate lives alone, and surmounted the stile that leads to the fields below the moors and tramped on past sheep in their coats ready for the coming winter. In these parts I expect it to be harsh and unforgiving.

A figure flits quickly past me, long narrow skirt skimming the grass, hood blown back by the wind. I glimpse the high-bridged nose and the pouting underlip and then she is gone ahead. I must be imagining it but I could swear I hear the name Keeper wafted into the wind.

Then the fields give way to the moors and I see on the skyline the outline of a massive black rock, perched high above the dips and hollows of the peaty verdure. A path winds up to it and I see some kind of aperture in the rock face, a narrow fissure that leads into blackness again.

Somewhere near here is the house I must find. I stand and look to east and west and then, emerging gradually from the swirling mist that has risen, I see for a moment a large building with narrow windows set deeply into mullions and a courtyard before it with a barred gate to deter unwelcome visitors. I take a step forward but the mist drops like a curtain between me and the dwelling and suddenly, in panic, I am turning and making my way back to the safety of the bustling street.

It was the year that the United Irishmen rose up against English rule that I jotted down in my journal, 'My father never loved my mother.'

Almost two years had gone by during which I had given my father little conscious thought but he still stalked in my dreams, dark, solitary, brooding, with the sudden twists of mood that had him curt and sharp, smiling, erupting into rage all the more frightening because it was at heart a cold rage that froze the senses.

There had been no additions to the Brunty family. But I never doubted that the loving remained strong between Ellis and Hugh. He still coughed when the wind blew from the north and the long golden ringlets for which she had been famed throughout the county were frosted with white like speckles of snow on golden broom, but their looks were as tender as they had ever been on the rare occasions I saw them. They were all in all to each other and united in their affection for their brood. Pat still taught away from the neighbourhood but came home at holiday season, paler and taller than ever in a black suit and shiny shoes. From the little I gathered during my rare visits to the Brunty house I had done him a favour with my act of spite for he was

52

well thought of by his employers and spoke often of going to England to study for one of the professions.

'He always was the brightest,' Ellis told me when I sat with her one summer afternoon in the field where she had been hanging washing to whiten. 'Not that the others are stupid, far from it! But there was always something special about Pat.'

Sometimes I thought she said such things because she hoped to remind me of the closing of the school but in fairness I think now that was never so. There was no spite in Ellis.

'What of the others?' I asked.

'William has left the village for a time as you may have heard.'

I had indeed heard and heard too that he had opened a *shibeen* in some village further south where he brewed his own liquor from corn and potatoes in defiance of the excisemen.

'Now don't frown like that, Miss Aspen,' Ellis said, speaking with some of her old friendliness. 'William will find his calling one day and meanwhile it's best he stay out of Imdel with the English soldiers still picking up people they thought joined in the rebellion.'

'They almost got William,' I said.

'Surrounding our house and threatening to burn it unless we told them where William was!' she nodded. 'And didn't my Hugh go out and speak to the Welsh sergeant in the old tongue, which is as near Welsh as makes them kissing cousins, and the sergeant marched his squad away and our William hidden in the thatch of the roof all the time!'

She laughed delightedly though the incident must have been a terrifying one.

'At least Hughie and James are earning an honest crust,' she resumed. 'Hiring themselves out to anyone who needs a willing heart and a strong pair of hands and Welsh is still at his books after the farm work is done! He wants to turn out a gentleman does our Welsh!'

I had wondered why Mr Brunty should name a son after the uncle who had mistreated him.

Now was not the moment to ask however for the little girls were running across to where we sat, seven-year-old Mary in the lead as usual, the twins Rose and Sarah skipping hand in hand, Alice toddling over the grass and Jane loitering at the rear, plainer and thinner than the rest with a look of pain about her childish mouth.

'My daughters,' Ellis said softly, and I felt her counting them off in her mind as birds are said to count their new-hatched eggs.

'And your joy,' I said, and she beamed at me.

'As your younglings will be one day when the right man comes.' She assured me.

'If,' I said, my indifference assumed as I stood up. 'Where will I find a mate round here?'

'Someone will come,' Ellis said. 'Someone always comes and the trick is to recognize the person and the moment.'

I gave her a brief, disbelieving smile and waved to the girls as I went back across the field. Behind me the scrubbed and mended garments danced on the gorse bushes in the summer sun.

A few days later, being of an enquiring mind, I went into the study where Mr Alistair was signing the accounts. He looked up with a faint air of surprise as I entered for I usually left him alone to get on with his task.

'Miss Aspen, is there anything you need of me?' he enquired.

'Some information.' I seated myself on one of the high-backed chairs and folded my hands in my lap.

'In particular?'

'My parents were married in Dublin?'

'With your grandfather and myself as witnesses, yes.'

'Their marriage lines are not in the desk,' I said.

Not by the flicker of a muscle did he betray surprise at the knowledge I had gone ferreting.

'One copy is in Dublin and the other in my own office,' he told me. 'Your grandfather thought that wiser since Mr Heathcliff was in and out of the place here and since your grandfather's death I have deemed it wiser to keep the document secure on my own premises.'

'With a copy of my grandfather's will,' I said.

'There are some people who will subvert law to their own ends,' Mr Alistair said. 'I protect your interests, Miss Aspen.'

'Mr Alistair, tell me about my father,' I said abruptly.

'I know little of him,' he said.

'Mr Alistair, I shall soon be seventeen,' I said impatiently. 'The same age my mother was when my father came into Ireland! I am not a small girl wanting a fairy-tale! Hugh Brunty brought him here—'

'An act of kindness he must later have regretted.'

'He was taken on by my grandfather and married my mother.'

'If you know that what else remains?' he asked.

'What else remains?' I echoed indignantly. 'I know my grandfather came here from the Highlands. That was after the first Jacobite Rebellion, which tells me he supported the Stuart cause though he never spoke of it! My father came from. . . ?'

'I have no idea and neither I believe has he,' Mr Alistair said. 'He looks like a gypsy and his voice betrays traces of the north of England but all he has ever said is that he was an orphan whose beginnings he has forgotten. As for his nature it is devious and intelligent and selfish. Your grandfather was a kindly soul who took him on and gave him more and more responsibility for which he was well paid.'

'And my mother helped him with his reading,' I prompted.

'He could already read and write but his education had been interrupted,' Mr Alistair said. 'How or why he never revealed.

55

Then one day, here with me accounting for some stock he'd purchased on the master's behalf – he was always very quick at figures – Miss Rosina came in. She had brought in a book she'd been reading to return it to the shelf and when she saw Mr Heathcliff she asked very sweetly if he would like to borrow it.'

'And?'

'He turned his sweetest smile upon her – in those days when he was yet a lad his smile had a sweetness in it – and said, "I fear the words were written for one more educated than I can claim to be."'

'And Miss Rosina said, quick as a flash, "I can supply the gaps if you don't object to taking instruction from a female."'

'He looked at her a moment as if he were regarding someone else and then he said, still with the sweetness of smile, "Females have already taught me a great deal, Miss Rosina, but I'd be grateful for a new instructor."'

'After that I often saw them together, walking about the garden or in the woods, one of them with a book in hand while the other listened attentively. I was fooled at first into thinking that he was truly grateful for her interest for he was all eager attention and, of course, by that time the master was entrusting him with more and more business. I was not the only one to be cozened.

'Then one day I came upon Miss Rosina in the garden. It was summer and the flowers were in bloom in the borders. She had picked a little nosegay and was tying them with a ribbon from her hair and as she stood there tying them up I saw tears coursing down her face and falling on the bright petals.

' "Miss Rosina, are you not well?" I enquired, for though she was lively and energetic she was never stout.

' "I am quite well," she answered, only half turning to look at me. "Heathcliff and I are to be wed, Mr Alistair."

' "Surely not!" I exclaimed, for the prospect of such an unequal match disturbed me greatly.

' "I hope to make him happy," she said, wiping away a tear

though others were spilling over. "Father has persuaded him to——"

'She could not speak further for sobbing but threw down the flowers and sped away, but not before I had seen plain on her arm the marks of bruising, and your grandfather was not a violent man.'

'Hugh Brunty said he did not ill-treat her!' I exclaimed.

'Hugh Brunty sees good in everything,' Mr Alistair said. 'After the marriage, on the rare occasions he was home, he did not handle her roughly as far as I know but your grandfather was vigilant. And Heathcliff was honest in his business dealings. It was to his advantage to be so.'

'What business?' I asked sharply.

'I am not privy to the details,' he said, and I saw from the swift downwards look he gave that he lied.

'And my grandfather paid him to wed my mother,' I said levelly. 'That was the way of it, wasn't it?'

'Your mother loved him and I've no reason to believe that he treated her harshly when they were married,' he said, and shut the books before him with an air of finality. 'If that is all, Miss Aspen, I have a busy working day ahead.'

'And you have still told me nothing about his origins,' I said.

'As to that you must ask him yourself the next time he comes,' Mr Alistair said. 'Good day to you, Miss Aspen.'

So much for that! As for my own beginnings, I saw them plainly. Rosina had loved him and he had made good use of the fact. I wondered, remembering the bruises on her arm, if he had forced her.

And I remembered too the ring of bird bones which I still wore, covered with a little pad of silk to protect its fragility. It was on my finger still as I sat thinking, and I rose at last and went up to my room and took it off and put it away in a little box because it was the only thing my father had given me and because my heart would no longer bear its weight.

FIVE

I walked a long way today over the moors, breathing in the mingled tints of faded green, burgundy and russet splashed with black under a pale sky. I passed several homesteads but none that resembled the house where my father lives and once I heard a shot and saw a grouse winged down into a hollow and stood watching as a dog streaked over to collect it but a moment later a ruddy cheeked man appeared, gun broken under his arm, and shouted to the dog, 'Here, Captain, here!'

Not Keeper then but Captain and the man, briefly saluting me, was already hidden by the curve of the hill.

I walked on towards the massive rock that rises blackly over the moor and, feeling an unaccustomed ache in my legs, climbed up the scree a little way and sat down in its shadow to rest. From this vantage point I could look around me in almost every direction and saw, about a half mile further on, high walls and barred gates that enclosed a park whose avenue and bridle paths were overhung with trees draped in autumn richness.

I could distinguish the outlines of a half-timbered mansion at the far side of a lawn only partly visible through the crowding trees and I surmised that the property must belong to one of the squires of the district. Or perhaps it was, after all, the house I sought.

In the other direction, mist was shutting out the sky and making the landscape a featureless blank. From above, higher than the nook I had chosen as temporary resting place, came the scrabble of feet descending and a man's voice, deep and tender with the faint overlay of a northern accent, 'Best let me go first lest you slip on the stones!'

'I'm as surefooted as you!' came the indignant, laughing reply. 'It's not so long since you were laid up with a wounded shoulder after tripping over your own fowling piece!'

'Seven months ago and I heal fast!' he retorted.

'Only because you have me to tend you!' the girl – it was a girl – replied.

They were descending rapidly now, passing me in my nook, not even glancing in my direction. I felt invisible as if I had become part of the heavy mist that now further compressed my view to the faint outlines of the high walls that barred entry to the leafy park with the mansion beyond.

The two skidded down the last bit of scree and stood, he holding her hands in his, the pair of them smiling at each other. They were so motionless that they reminded me of two figures in a painting torn from its frame.

I saw them in profile and they were both young, he in his early twenties with dark hair curling over a forehead that was broad rather than high, his eyes steadfastly regarding the slender girl in her green riding dress and cloak whose hood had crumpled to her shoulders to reveal long ringlets of palest gold.

The young man bore a fleeting resemblance to a picture I have long carried in my mind, of a dark-haired boy muttering the name of his lost love in a Dublin hostelry.

Time ran backwards faster when he said, still holding her hands, 'We'd best get the horses, Catherine, or they might stray in this mist and then Mrs Dean will be anxious.'

'And Joseph swear at us for a pair of nowts!' she replied, and taking a step nearer to her escort, wound both her arms about his neck and kissed him lingeringly.

'Tomorrow we'll go to the Grange and start making plans for the arranging of the furniture and the airing of the linen,' he said, having given her back her kiss with interest.

'There are the horses!' she cried. 'Looking for us!'

'You credit the beasts with more intelligence than they possess,' he answered, laughing.

'I credit everything with more intelligence than they possess, even you!' she retorted, slipping from his grasp and seeming to spring away into the mist behind.

I heard her high bright laughter pealing through the air and then he strode after her and I saw them, dimly entwined, as they went to catch their mounts and heard the clip-clopping of hoofs as they remounted and gained the rutted track that wound past the great rock to the walls that barred trespassers from the manor house.

I rose stiffly from my perch and went down to level ground again. The manor house was not far distant and the mist, now that I moved through it, not so thick. I made up my mind on the spot and walked boldly along the path to the gates. They were barred but not locked and by dint of slipping my hand through and sliding the bar across, I gained entry.

The house had appeared nearer than it really was, for once within the gates I saw the path curve and divide in several directions. It had markers of white stone at intervals presumably to guide the visitor but the paths themselves diverged widely, some dipping amid the trees with the very last of the autumn fruits on them, others leading to buildings that were obviously outhouses and stables.

I took the path that seemed to bend towards the roofs that were still visible above the descending mist and found myself after nearly twenty minutes in a yard with overflowing dustbins

and the smell of rotting meat. The gable-end of the main building was in view however, with a wicker gate between me and
what must surely be more salubrious surroundings. I leaned to
unhasp the latch and shut the gate behind me as I found myself
opposite a side door.

When I pressed down the handle the door opened, affording
me sight of a narrow hallway.

I raised my voice slightly to halloo and heard its echo, thin
and quavering, bounce back at me from the surrounding walls.

The house felt empty or rather as if I was the only living soul
within. Beyond the walls and the flight of steps ahead of me I
pictured empty rooms filled with shapes that turned and twisted
in the unbreathed air. I opened a door at the foot of the stairs
that showed me a kitchen, neat enough but with no signs of food
being prepared or water boiled. After a moment's thought I shut
the door and went up the stairs that curved on to a wide landing with doors all around me.

This house was bigger than my grandfather's dwelling, the
walls wainscoted, the floors of shining wood with rugs rolled up
against the walls and furniture shrouded beneath white dust-
sheets. Had I stood still for a little while I think shapes would
have begun to stir under their white coverings but I moved on
rapidly, opening doors and venturing within.

The air itself was icy, as if a layer of frost lay over the house,
and drew patterns on the windows forbidding sunshine to enter.

In one bedroom the indentation of a head on a pillow made
me start nervously as if its owner were in the adjoining dressing-
room where a couple of mangy wigs occupied wooden,
featureless headstands.

A lawyer or a magistrate had lived here once? I went into the
next room and saw a whip laid as if abandoned across a foot-
stool and a pile of laundry tied up ready for the basket.

In another room I found leather upholstered seats and rows

of books, their bindings roughly dusted but still holding smears. A desk held some blank sheets of paper and an inkwell innocent of ink.

The great house was deserted. The two I had seen on the moor planned to live here then? It was not a prospect I envied them for the cold alone would freeze love to death before it was fully awake and aware. Perhaps all houses were like this when left vacant for two months or more, like the bones of birds denuded of their flesh and feathers.

A wider, more gracious staircase fell to the ground floor from the landing. I went down it cautiously, seeing the balustrade newly burnished and the treads radiant with rubbing. In the lower hall the doors stood open and I looked into a dining-room with a massive table along which bowls and vases were ranged, obviously just taken from the glass fronted cupboards whose shelves betrayed dust outlining where the ornaments had stood.

There was a small parlour with curtains of faded rose and a *chaise-longue* like the picture of one I had seen in a book, and a room filled with boxes stuffed with papers and old magazines, some stained with what looked like seawater, and another chamber in which sketches of horses hung on the walls. And over all was the unmistakable aura of . . . not exactly decay, but something subtler and more insidious.

A narrow staircase led up out of this latter room and I mounted to a door which admitted me to a pretty bedchamber, with a frieze of mermaids around the walls but with bed stripped to its wood, and chest of drawers and wardrobe empty with doors hanging motionless in the still air.

I pulled open the drawers wider but there was nothing there save a tiny key taped to the back of one.

'There is a narrow drawer right at the bottom,' grandfather had said to me once – at a Christmastide I think. 'It has no betraying signs save a keyhole under the upper rim. You may keep your most private treasures there when you are older, love letters, whatever!'

I prised out the key and knelt to fit it into the hidden hole, wondering whose grandfather or parents had given such a gift and to whom.

Inside the recess, fragile under my hand as I slipped in my fingers and slid it out, was a sheet of paper, somewhat yellowed but with the writing on its inner surfaces still clear; the hand-writing itself pointed with two blots as if the writer had shed a tear before folding it.

For a moment I hesitated and then I began to read.

Dearest Edgar and Catherine,

Forgive me if you find this and read it. I love him so greatly that my mind will hold nothing else! He fills me to the brim. I know you will be angry and you, my sweet Catherine furious, but I am harnessed by my heart and cannot save myself. Be happy together and try with all the goodness in you both to think of me as your sister still,

Isabella

I read the spidery message again, my brow creased in thought. Isabella? Written perhaps fifteen or twenty years ago to judge from its faint brown tinge, and it had been written by someone who is drawn against her better judgement into an alliance. I had no way of knowing who the man with whom this Isabella had eloped might be, but the name of Catherine had set my nerves jangling. And my father told me he had wed a second time after my own mother died.

I put the note in my pocket and relocked the hidden drawer and put the key back in its place, though the tape refused to stick properly, and went down the stairs again.

Baize-padded doors led obviously to the kitchen and I turned into the one remaining room. It was also the largest with double doors folded back at the far end to display yet another chamber with a daybed in it and a portrait hanging on the wall. It had been one of two for I could spot the faint discolouration where a second frame had hung. I went over to look at it for I had seen no other portraits in the house.

A young man with long light hair curling to his shoulders and large eyes set in a handsome countenance smiled out from a pale background.

He looked, I mused, all gentleness, but there was no energy in his lineaments, no sparkle in the blue eyes. Yet there was a hint of obstinacy about the mouth and something in the set of the beardless jaw that hinted at strong emotions held in check by a calm, indomitable will.

There were quick light footsteps along the hall and before I could move, a girl walked in. For an instant I began to compose some kind of apology for trespassing but though she looked in my direction she took no more notice of me than if I had been part of the furniture. Indeed, as I stepped hastily aside she came straight up to the portrait and stood, her full skirted gown swirling about her ankles, and gazed up at the portrait with painful intensity as if she willed that disembodied head to float from its frame and join her.

There was a look about her of the girl I had seen by the black rocks on the moor for she was about the same age and had the same long fair ringlets but a second look showed me she had more in common with the portrait itself. The same languid blue eyes and the same obstinate jut of the mouth proved a near relationship.

She remained, apparently rooted to the spot for several minutes, and then as swiftly turned and without vouchsafing me so much as a glance, went back the way she had arrived, feet tapping on the wooden floor.

Not until the last echo of her walking had diminished into the distance and I heard the soft shutting of a door did I realize that her face upturned to her painted companion had brought forth no reflection in the glass that protected the picture though my own face had been shadowed forth there when I had studied it.

I could hear voices, chattering in the odd, drawling dialect I have heard in this corner of the land, and I stepped hastily to the windows to look out. A group of women, aprons tied around their waists, pails in their hands, were walking to the side of the house where the kitchen was situated, obviously returned from some business in the village before they resumed their house-cleaning operations.

A casement was unhasped. I opened it wider and put my legs over the sill from where it was but a few feet to the ground. The women had all vanished round the gable-end of the building but I didn't venture to explore further lest my boldness lead to discovery. Instead I walked rapidly across the somewhat untended lawn to the main gates and passed through unchallenged and unseen.

The moors were clear now though wisps of mist lingered in the still green hollows. Against the sky the black rocks reared up like some prehistoric monster that both threatens and guards its territory.

If the great house I had just invaded belonged to my father then it is his no longer. It is untenanted, save for the servants who come to set it in order, save too perhaps for the pale-haired girl who leaves no shadow of herself upon glass.

I began the long walk back to the village, wishing I had acted on my first resolution and hired a mount but all my life I have been used to walking in the countryside. This, I mused, as I plodded through tangled grass and avoided the streams that bubbled below the surface of an occasional peaty spot of marsh, was more like foreign territory.

Perhaps my father has left the house because the pale-haired girl walks there rather too often. I find that hard to believe because in our few encounters he has always given me the impression that he is a man of strong nerves and practical good sense.

Yet even Brigit, who is sensible, believes that the Sidhe dwell in the caves around Imdel, and once in an unguarded moment she told me that not many weeks before my mother died she heard the banshee.

'As Our Blessed Lady is my witness,' she told me, 'I took a bit of a walk in the grounds one light evening for Miss Rosina – Mrs Heathcliff I should say – had eaten an early supper and retired with a book to her room, and I needed a breath of fresh air.

'It was a fine late summer evening with twilight stealing the sun from over the hills and I was walking along thinking of nothing in particular when I heard a sound – Mother of God! how it startled me! A long, low wailing like the torments of a soul in hell! I stood still, telling myself that some animal must be trapped in a snare, but no stoat or rabbit would wail in that fashion.

'After a few moments the wailing turned to a kind of sobbing, almost human in the feeling behind it, and I hurried on for fear some poor soul needed help. Then it stopped as suddenly as it had begun and, as I paused also, Mr Heathcliff came towards me, striding rapidly, turning away his face and not attempting any greeting; not that I expected any, for the man, for all his industry and his getting round Mr Stewart to marry Miss Rosina, is a ruffian right down to the place where other people keep their hearts.

'I went on a little further but the noises had stopped and I wasn't sorry to turn back towards the house and the warm safe rooms.'

'Perhaps it was my father?' I had suggested.

'Invoking his own father: the devil!' she said. 'No, *macushla*, no being born of womankind made that sound. It was the banshee!'

I left the black rocks behind me and struck out in the direction of the village again, promising myself that I would make a good supper and make enquiries about the great house as soon as I reached the hostelry.

I slowed my pace now and then to look back but apart from the waving grasses and the sheep in their greyish coats there were no other people to be seen. This is not, I feel, a country where neighbours greet strangers as friends as we do in Ireland, but a land which, despite its expanse of moor and bog, is closed in upon itself, impervious to outside influences. Or perhaps the land itself nourishes them, feeding hearts and minds, rooting them to the earth.

I was passing a broad stream that gushed down over rocks to a deep pool fringed by fern. There were large stones placed across the widest part of the stream and a figure I had begun to recognize sat on the highest one, booted feet dangling over the stone above the water.

I knew the face, seen briefly by lamplight, seen again in profile and now bent over a book of some kind on which she was writing.

I was determined that this time I would not be ignored and so stood and called across the width of the stream, above the rushing of the waters, 'Excuse me but am I bound in the right direction for the village?'

For a moment I thought she hadn't heard for she continued to write and then, placing her hand flat across the page, she lifted her head, her eyes sliding away from me and said in a musical tone marred by the curtness of her utterance.

'Follow the path and you'll arrive there, sooner or later.'

I was about to embark on a further utterance – I cannot think what it would have been – when she slewed around until her back was towards me and began writing again.

I bit my lip and walked on, wishing I had asked about her dog, asked why the curate had told me that he lived alone, yet aware that even had I enquired it was unlikely I would have received a civil or satisfactory answer. At least she was real, for when I looked back I saw that she was still there, head bent over the page, left hand writing busily.

The inhabitants of this land are as rude and uncultured as the land itself. Strange then that I should feel myself to be already a part of them like an alien thread stitched into a tapestry.

When I reached the inn I came upstairs to change my boots which were sadly begrimed from tramping the moor and rang for the servant, giving her instructions to have them cleaned and telling her that I would like a pot of strong coffee and some toast in the snug.

'I can bring thee the vittles mesen, Miss,' she asserted. 'Moll is gone ower t'Thrushcross Grange t'do a bit of mucking oot theer.'

I nodded and proceeded to change into a lighter gown and a pair of low-heeled slippers neat enough for indoors but useless outside. My hair I tied back loosely, postponing any combing out of the tangles.

The public bar was quiet save for a couple of farmers talking crop yields when I descended the stairs. I went through to the snug and found the woman had been as good as her word, setting the coffee pot on one of the tables and bringing in a plate of hot buttered toast as I sat down.

'I seem to be the only one eating,' I commented. 'The visitors are not all gone?'

'No Miss,' she said. 'Mr Lockwood went south again and three of the travelling gentlemen left this morning but there's allus a few folk int'place even when summer's on't turn.'

'Mr Lockwood was staying here?' I said. 'He seemed a very polite gentleman.'

'Very polite, Miss,' she agreed. 'He wasn't here above two or three nights though. He rented Thrushcross Grange last year but niver stayed long. Seemingly he came back into these parts t'settle the rent.'

'Is Thrushcross Grange the large dwelling with a fine park about it past the great black rocks?'

'Aye, Miss, it is. I niver were there mysen but it's a fine property they do say.'

'And the black rocks?' I questioned.

'That'd be Penistone Crag, Miss. They do say there's a fairy cave up there where a strange sort of folk come and go, but I've niver climbed them mesen.'

'The Beautiful Ones,' I murmured and thought of the caves round Imdel where Brigit had sworn the Sidhe dwelt.

'I wouldn't be knawing that, Miss,' said she, looking slightly puzzled. 'There are plenty of strange tales round these parts. For mesen I disbelieve half on 'em and don't pay heed to th'rest.'

'You are not from Gimmerton then?'

Her accent was softer than I had so far heard, easier to follow.

'I'm from Halifax way, Miss,' she answered.

'That's a coal-mining town, isn't it?' I vaguely remembered heaps of slurry along the road as we passed in the coach.

'Aye, Miss, though there's some round Gimmerton too,' she replied. 'Hereabouts is mainly sheep and cattle. Will that be all, Miss?'

'Do sit down for a moment,' I invited. 'What brought you here?'

'My man died of the coughing sickness.' For an instant her hands plucked at the edge of her apron and then she went on, 'I'd no bairns and work int'mines is hard, pulling them great carts underground and not sae mich int'payment, so I came ower tae Gimmerton two months since and got a room and now I hire mesen out when anyone's off poorly or getting wed or some sich foolishness. I clean for t'curate too now and then.'

'The Reverend Charnock? He lives alone?'

'Aye, he does,' she nodded. 'Quiet man, not th'soart t'marry. Likes his books and getting up int'pulpit t'read his sermons. And that parsonage is a grand big building, needs a family and a passel of childer running around!'

'You know most people in the village then?'

'Mostly by sight, Miss. They'm close in these parts, keep themselves tae themselves like.'

'And Thrushcross Grange?' I set down my piece of toast. 'Who owns it?'

'Oh, that'd be Mrs Linton, Miss,' she said. 'She's widowed but getting ready to wed again at New Year and moving theer so all must be made ready. If tha'll pardon me, Miss, I've glasses t'wash before t'bar fills up. It gets right crowded after sunset! Enjoy tha vittles, Miss.' She bobbed a curtsy and hurried out.

I stared after her, crumbling bits of toast between my fingers. She had already imbibed something of the nature of the people here, I thought irritably. She had not taken my offer of a chair and in her face when I mentioned Thrushcross Grange something had shut down, a barrier against strangers.

I rose and went upstairs again to find my boots neatly polished outside the door.

Now I sit before my journal with the last entry in it before me, the letters black and sharp on the white page. 'My father has told me to visit him.'

That and nothing more.

SIX

In the September of 1800 I reached the age of nineteen, an age that seemed to me immeasurably older than any I had known before. I was gradually establishing myself as mistress of my estate, causing Brigit to shake her head and grumble that she might as well retire because I was seizing the reins and leaving her with no occupation.

'You deserve a rest,' I told her. 'You're no longer a young woman you know.'

'And may all your bairns be born naked for that remark!' she cried indignantly. 'Holy Mother of God, but when did I rear you to insult the old?'

To stop her muttering I told Mr Alistair that her wages were to be increased and that she was to retain the right of hiring and firing servants – though most of them had been with us since I was a child and few were ever dismissed from service.

The harvest had been scanty that year with blight spreading as the rains poured out like great jets from the overloaded sky and in parts of Ireland I heard of hunger, caused not only by ill weather but by the land agents who thought nothing of turfing out a family when the rent payment was late or the increase could not be met.

'We will keep the rents at the old level,' I told Mr Alistair when he was checking the books one day. 'I'll not throw our own people into the mire for the sake of a little profit! At least I can set my own rates without the English looking over my shoulder!'

'You'll lose profit that way,' he warned.

'The other businesses – the business my father undertook for my grandfather,' I hazarded. 'That still pays well?'

'That's dealt with in Dublin,' he answered, shutting up the books somewhat hastily.

'And my father tends to it?'

'I believe that when your parents married two-thirds of the business was handed over to Mr Heathcliff,' he said stiffly. 'He moved his field of operations into Yorkshire. With your share I have nothing to do. An agent deals with that part. So far I understand he has proved honest and takes only his stipend. I think that is all for today, Miss Stewart.'

He bade me good day and left, mounting up as stiffly as he had spoken, and it occurred to me that he too was ageing. Despite his formal manners and his belief that no female was to be trusted near a rent roll I was fond of him because he had been part of my life for as long as I could remember.

It seemed to me suddenly as if everybody about me was ageing fast even as I turned to look at them. Brigit grumbled about the labour of overseeing the younger maids who were apt to dawdle and giggle as they folded the laundry or peeled the potatoes and the trouble some caused her by slipping out to meet their sweethearts after dark, though had I taken away one jot of her authority she would have spat fire!

I had no laundry to fold and no sweetheart to meet. At the centre of my life was a void not yet filled. Sometimes I laid idle plans to travel into Scotland and find out if I'd any kin there, but the newspapers spoke of harsh poverty as the landlords imposed enclosure on the highlands and took themselves and their wives to Edinburgh to live like lords in that great city.

I had celebrated my birthday two months before though cele-
brate is hardly the most appropriate word to describe the small
gifts the servants gave me and the iced cake which I invited
Brigit to share. Part of me longed for music and dancing and
strong arms about me and part of me knew that unless my soul-
mate came I would remain solitary.

In that mood on a chilly November morning I rode Jackdaw
down into the glen which was sodden still with rain, the turf
spongy and the rocks dyed a darker grey by the downpours.

Hugh Brunty was there, a creel of fish in one hand, and he
waved at me as I drew rein and squelched across to lay a hand
on Jackdaw's neck as he greeted me.

'At least the rains have swollen the rivers and brought the fish
further upstream,' he said in his quietly cheerful fashion. 'Many
a family will be glad of a fish supper tonight. There's nothing so
tasty as a fresh herring cooked in a cornmeal crust with a few
taties on the side!'

'Are you all managing?' I asked hesitantly, slipping from the
pony's back and standing on a slightly drier piece of ground.

'Better than many,' he answered with a slight cloud coming
over his pleasant features. 'There are hundreds burnt out of
their homes during the past two or three years for having risen
up against the English.'

'But your house was not burned,' I reminded him.

'Only because the sergeant of the troop was a Welshman,' he
answered with a grin. 'Aye, they may pay lip-service to England
but we're all Celts under the skin!'

'Well, I am Scots on my mother's side,' I said. 'I do wonder
sometimes about my father's line.'

'A tangled one I'd say,' he replied. 'Part Romany I'd guess and
maybe a dash of the Irish and maybe a Lascar jumped over his
grandmother's wall long years ago – begging your pardon, Miss
Aspen!'

'He came to Ireland when he was a very young man.'

'I reckon he smuggled himself aboard the first ship he found,' Hugh Brunty said thoughtfully. 'Not coming towards something but fleeing from something else. He never said, which makes me think he's not so much of the Irish in him for we Irish will gab for hours but he was silent from the start.'

'Though he muttered the name of Cathy you said.'

'Aye, so he did. Moaned it rather than muttered in a manner that might have betokened love or hate. He's not ridden in, has he?'

I shook my head.

'I thought he might have come around the time of my birthday but he never did,' I told him. 'It's four years since he was last here.'

'You mark the years of his absence?'

'Ever since he came on the day my grandfather died,' I said, 'I have felt his presence – faint when he's not here like a pool settling into smoothness again after a stone has been spun into its centre, and when I have seen him the pool stirs with hidden life that writhes and twists in the shallows of my mind like the stone spinning down into weeds at the deepest part of the pool.'

'And I brought him here,' Hugh Brunty said wryly. 'A good deed doesn't always bear sound fruit, Miss Aspen. Let's talk of other things!'

'Is your wife well?' I asked politely, not wanting to talk of other things.

'Beautiful as she ever was!' His face lit with enthusiasm. 'My Ellis is so far beyond other women that some nights I just lean on my elbow and trace her features in my mind, dwelling on each blessed part of her.'

'And is she. . . ?'

'Breeding again? No!' He looked at me and laughed.

'Alice must be three now,' I said.

'Four and she's the last of them. Ten is enough for any man and Ellis is close on forty and tires more rapidly than a colleen might do, so we decided our family was complete. At night—' He shot me a teasing glance. 'At night she sleeps and I draw her in my mind. Love is not only of the flesh, Miss Aspen. But you'll find that out for yourself when the right man comes along.'

'One's not likely to arrive here looking for an Aspen Stewart,' I said gloomily.

'One day you might go in search of him,' he answered.

'Or put an advertisement in the newspaper? No, thank you! I shall remain a happy spinster and knit stockings for mermaids to wear,' I said lightly.

At my side Jackdaw gave an impatient little snicker.

'Not long now, old lady!' Hugh Brunty brought out a piece of carrot and offered it to her. 'She still has some vigour in her, Miss Aspen, but she's losing weight a mite.'

'I don't ride her far,' I said defensively.

'Aye, there's a kindness in you that you get from your mother, may God rest her sweet soul!' he said.

'Was my father kind to my mother?' I said abruptly.

'I wasn't privy to their private moments, but I never heard of any cruelty,' he said. 'Will you walk over and take a bite of herring with us and I'll walk back with you later?'

'I'd best not or Brigit will twitter,' I said regretfully.

'Then I'll be on my own way. Oh, we'd a letter from Pat the other day – a real, properly franked letter from Dublin. He is thinking of sitting the examinations for Cambridge University in a year or two if he can get his Greek up to standard. He may be home for a few days at Christmas too. His mother will be glad to see him again, as will I.'

'And the rest?' I still felt slightly awkward when Pat was mentioned.

'William's courting it seems,' he said, looking pleased as he always did when asked for news of his family. 'One of the Shaw girls: a nice family. Hugh and James are finding life tough with the bad weather hindering road building or bridge mending. Welsh will be joining them once he turns sixteen. The girls can help me on the farm.'

'Why did you name your son Welsh when the uncle of that name was so unkind to you?' I asked curiously. 'It cannot be a name of which you want to be reminded.'

'After our first four lads were born and named,' he told me, 'the fifth came out dark as a wizard and smaller than the rest. It was Ellis who said, "a name isn't affected by the person who bears it and this babe may bring the name honour instead of unhappy memories", so we named him so and he's a bright boy.'

'And your bad uncle?'

'There was a tale he fell into the fire when he was drunk but I never went back to see,' he told me. 'I'll be getting on, Miss Aspen. Visit when you've a mind!'

He nodded to me and went off, the creel heavy in his hand, and for a moment I envied him his bright, snug home and the wife who loved him beyond the desires of flesh. Then I led Jackdaw into higher, drier ground, remounted and trotted home.

There was a tall figure standing on the front steps and if one's heart can sink and leap in the same moment then mine did.

'So here's an errant daughter!' Mr Heathcliff said as I dismounted and called to the groom to take my pony. 'Never here to welcome your daddy!'

'You never send word when you're coming,' I replied.

I offered my cheek politely but he flicked it with his gloves, saying, 'And when did we go in for soft kissing? Save them for your sweetheart, for they're wasted on me!'

'I have no sweetheart,' I said loftily. 'Where are you staying?'

'Here, if you will have me,' he answered to my surprise. 'Oh,

I'm aware I have no claim on your hospitality but God knows I grow weary of inns and your Irish ones are dirtier than most.'

'You were glad of a bed when Hugh Brunty gave you his,' I said, going ahead of him into the hall.

'Aye, and fools like Brunty will never rise in the world,' he said, following me.

Brigit entered from the servants' quarters, hackles risen, and shot him a darkling look.

'Is Mr Heathcliff to be lodged here, Miss Aspen?' she asked.

'Have a room made ready and send us some food into the dining-room,' I bade her.

'You'll be requiring a long spoon then,' she muttered.

To my surprise Mr Heathcliff drew her towards him and implanted a smacking kiss on her cheek.

'One day I'll introduce you to Ellen Dean,' he said with a laugh. 'You and she are made from the same mould and God knows she's pure porcelain!'

'Who is Ellen Dean?' I asked, going after him into the dining-room.

'A housekeeper who has stood my friend more than once.'

'I am glad you have friends.'

'I have people who are useful to me,' he replied harshly, his good humour evaporating.

'Will you have something to drink before we eat?' I asked, somewhat belatedly remembering my manners. 'Whiskey, brandy?'

'A brandy in the evening is the sum total of my imbibing,' he answered, gazing round moodily as if he sought to recapture memory. 'I have seen drunkenness at first hand and resolved early in life never to fall prey to that temptation though I've helped another along that road, not that Hindley needed much helping.'

'Hindley?'

'A boyhood companion,' he replied, giving the two words a twist as sour as lemons. 'A foster brother if you will. Have you raised your rents?'

'No, nor will I,' I said.

'Why not?'

'The people cannot afford to pay more and would be driven out and then I'd get nothing at all.'

'You've a sound head on your shoulders,' he approved.

'And I will not send more hardship where hardship already wears the crown.'

'And a sentimental heart in your breast!' he said with a down-curving grin. 'Cultivate the first and root up the second and you'll do for me.'

'As long as I do for myself I shall be happy,' I told him.

'A simple formula! I wish you joy in its fulfilment! Are we to be fed today or no?'

He crossed to the bell-rope and jerked it impatiently just as two of the maids brought in cold meats and bread and a dish of roasted potatoes.

'Please join me.' I seated myself at the head of the table and saw his winged brows shoot upwards.

'Am I to sit here then?' he enquired, going to the foot of the table. 'Then our talk will have to be shouted and all our private business made known.'

'I doubt we have private business to transact,' I said. 'You may sit where you please!'

The maids had hurried out, warned no doubt by Brigit not to linger. From the foot of the long table he regarded me with amusement for a moment, then in a couple of long strides he reached where I sat, whirled me out of my seat and held me by both wrists in a bruising grasp that made me wince with pain though I was too proud to cry aloud.

'Never seek to command me!' he said through gritted teeth.

'I am not one to be set down, Aspen Stewart! Remember that otherwise I will take a father's privilege and teach you better manners! And don't try to kick my shins again as you did last time! I am not a man who takes pleasure in female violence except for – oh, but she might have trampled me into blood and bone and I'd've kissed the hem of her skirt!'

I sank into my seat again, rubbing my wrists as he released me and took the chair on my left, half turning away to cover his face with his hand as if he struggled with some deadly emotion of which he was half shamed but held him relentlessly.

I busied myself with serving out meat and the potatoes while he mastered whatever devil held him in thrall until he gave a couple of shivering sighs and sat down, his dark face as impassive as if someone had wiped it clear of every emotion.

'You ought not to play games with me,' he said at last. 'I am not a playful man, Aspen. Surely you've learnt that by now?'

'How can I learn anything?' I answered sulkily. 'You hardly ever come into Ireland and then I suspect it's only to seek out the value of my property!'

'Which is yours entirely, my dear!' He displayed his white teeth in a sardonic grin. 'As I am not in any position to cheat you then I will take care that nobody else does. I daresay the estate accounts are locked up tightly?'

'Mr Alistair keeps a firm grip on them,' I said. 'When I am twenty-one I will have the right to order everything as I wish and meanwhile they are safe in his hands. You needn't fret about my welfare.'

'Did you think that I ever did?' he asked, surprise in his tone.

'Yes,' I answered slowly. 'I think you do take an interest in my welfare because of the estate but also because there is something of yourself in me. Not out of affection but—'

'Affection! What nimby pimby words you use!' he interrupted with a grimace. 'Affection!'

'You feel none for anybody?' I ventured.

'None for anybody that walks alive upon this earth. I've a reluctant respect for Mrs Dean who showed me some small kindness from time to time. The rest I'd sooner hang!'

'The rest?' I looked at him sharply. 'You spoke of a son you had never seen. . . ?'

'Linton.' He looked at the piece of meat he was conveying to his mouth and laid his fork down again. 'Yes, Linton lives with me now, his mother having packed her bags and departed heavenwards. What a propensity my wives have for dying on me!'

'Then he is now . . . how old?'

'Sixteen. He was born in the same month you were.'

'Do you accord well together?'

'Oh, we are a devoted father and son,' he said with a sneer. 'He's a fair, frail thing with the guts of a jellyfish and the coughing sickness already upon him. But he'll be a happy husband before he dies.'

'He's to be wed so young?' I said in surprise.

'Oh, he'll be married and buried within a short space,' he said brutally. 'I've a pretty bride in mind for him. A niece of mine by marriage who will suit him very well.'

'Have you any blood relatives?' I asked boldly.

'None that I know. Why?'

'You have me!'

'And what a treasure you are proving to be to me, my pet!' He put out a hand and pulled not ungently at my hair. 'God, but if you were a lad I might mate you to great advantage!'

'I've no wish to be wedded,' I said.

'And what a liar you are proving to be! There's hot blood in you somewhere and you didn't get it from your mother. Anyway I have the first glimmerings of a notion in my mind – well, not quite the first for they have lain dormant in me for a long time – but there's a lad—'

'A blood relation?'

'How you do harp upon the blood!' he marvelled. 'No, he is a foster nephew in a way. A fine-looking young man sunk in animal ignorance which is his reward for having a father who kept me from my books and turned me into a bond slave!

'A bright boy whom I have turned into something not much better than a beast of the fields, illiterate, uncouth and – here is the joke of it – most damnably fond of me for I've been virtual father and mother to him since he was a toddling sprat. His father misused me so I misuse the son and he hasn't a notion of it! That's the best part of the joke! He has no idea that he is intelligent.'

'You may forget about your foster nephew,' I said, 'for I would not mate with one such as that, and you need not trouble to lose your temper for you may strike me but you'll not alter my mind!'

'We shall see,' was all he said, but I saw the cold gleam in the dark eyes and wished that he had not come again into Ireland.

We finished the meal in silence and I rang the bell for the table to be cleared away. Mr Heathcliff had risen and was walking restlessly up and down the room and I saw Brigit peep in at the door and scuttle away again just as he turned.

'You have still told me nothing of your own beginnings,' I said as he made an about turn and came towards me again.

'I remember nothing of them,' he said. 'No, that's the truth. I was seven years old when I was taken in by a man who treated me as a son, even named me after a previous son who had died in babyhood.'

'Then how do you know you were seven?'

'Seven or thereabouts.' He shrugged indifferently. 'I have one vague memory of a woman with tiny apples tied to the end of her plaits but nothing more at all save for voices shouting and blows raining and a dark closet with spiders' webs stretched across the wall and the feel of them on my face. And after that a cold ride and a warm kitchen.'

'And you never wanted to find out?'

He shook his head.

'I found my soul in that warm place,' he said and for a moment his expression softened and I saw the eager boy leap into life behind his eyes. 'She was – is all I ever desired, ever hungered after, but she betrayed me through her own greed and selfishness. I forgave her her sin but she died of it all the same. For a lad of sixteen or seventeen betrayal is the ultimate offence.'

'Then it was a long time ago,' I ventured.

'It was twenty years ago,' he rejoined. 'It was yesterday and it is today and it will be tomorrow. It will never end until—'

I could feel pity rising in me and crushed it down within myself, saying instead, 'Some people would have killed themselves and followed after.'

'Oh, I'd scores to settle first!' he said with a mirthless smile. 'And how am I to know if she'd be waiting for me if I cheated fate and took my own road out? No, this purgatory is a kind of test of my faithfulness and hers, for I'll swear she suffers too. I want her to suffer!'

I sat mute, knowing he spoke of the Cathy for whom he had moaned in his sleep in the Dublin inn. I dared say nothing for his mood altered so rapidly. Sometimes I felt that he was unable to help himself and at other times I saw calculation in every word and gesture.

'Enough of these sentimental meanderings!' he said abruptly, the sudden jollity in his tone striking a false note. 'Tell me about yourself, Aspen Stewart! You are virtually your own mistress now, are you not? You can raise rents and order the meals and ride like a lady on that pony of yours who should have been sent to the knacker's yard a year or two ago!'

'Jackdaw holds up well,' I said stiffly.

'And you grow into a handsome young woman! Yes, you have fire and spirit in you, daughter. Those you inherit from me so be content with that and stop asking questions about dark beginnings that cannot be told! Would you object to my looking over the account books now?'

'Mr Alistair—' I began.

'Has copies in his office. I know that, but when I worked for your grandfather the originals were lodged in the desk in the study. Have you the key?'

I handed it over silently, deeming it useless to protest. He took it with a slight smile.

'Come! You shall supervise,' he said, leading the way. 'Believe it or not, but I've no desire to steal from your fortune for I've plenty of my own including a bundle of shares that would astonish you.'

In the study he took out the books and sat, chin on hand, as he studied them closely.

'It looks as if Alistair has not played you false,' he said at last. 'That pleases me and astonishes me for if you ever want to employ a criminal find yourself a lawyer. You ought to raise your rents a little though just to remind your tenants that you have the power. Oh, you do not come fully into your own until you are of age but already Alistair is in the habit of gaining your approval for any new scheme.'

'Would you like to inspect the servants' quarters next?' I asked. 'Peer into the larder and the stillroom? Or check the maids make their beds and empty their chamberpots in the mornings?'

'The domestic side I will leave to you!' He piled the books back into the drawer, locked it and tossed me the key.

'Will you tell me something?' I said.

'How prettily you ask!' He turned to look at me. 'Not more about my illustrious descent I trust?'

84

'There is another side to the estate not directly allied to it,' I said. 'My grandfather employed you as agent and handed over two thirds to you when you wed my mother. The business is carried on in Dublin.'

'And Liverpool. They are both ports you know.'

'What is the nature of the business?' I asked.

'Nothing illegal if that's what you were fearing!' He sent me a sardonic grin. 'Neither need you concern yourself with the details. Your grandfather came out of the Highland wastes with almost nothing and died a rich man on the profits from the Dublin–Liverpool business.'

'If you are importing slaves!' I said.

'What a vivid imagination you have!' he marvelled. 'No, black cargo is too expensive to import and since the troubles with France even cognac and lace are hazardous cargoes to carry when one breaks the blockade. No, the business is legal and brings great peace of mind to many people though I'd warn you not to experiment with its benefits yourself! Now you have asked as many questions as I intend answering and I mean to retire to the room Brigit has obviously lovingly prepared for me and read for a little.'

'My mother helped you,' I said impulsively and blushed for my lack of tact.

'She did indeed though I was hardly illiterate when I arrived here. I seldom trouble myself with books these days but I devour the shipping news and the value of various properties. I will see you this evening.'

He went out and I heard his tread ascending the stairs.

Brigit came in shortly afterwards, lowering her voice as she shut the door.

'How long does he mean to stay?' she asked.

'He may stay as short or as long as he pleases,' I told her. 'I can hardly turn my own father out of doors.'

'He never should've been let indoors in the first place,' she said in a grumbling whisper. 'Mother of God, Miss Aspen, but he's here for no good purpose! The day Hugh Brunty brought him here was a bad day for us all!'

'He was a boy,' I said coolly.

'Aye, and the devil himself once wore petticoats!' she retorted.

'We are speaking of my father,' I reminded her coldly. 'He is my only relative as far as I know. Had he not come here I would not have been born! You take too much on yourself!'

'And when he comes,' she said, 'he sharpens you as a whetstone sharpens a knife and shaves off your kindliness like flecks of rust.'

'We shall sup here later on the small table,' I broke in. 'And I want something better than cold cuts and potatoes. There is a whole cured ham in the pantry that's not been touched and a goose too fat to spare until Christmas. And I shall wear my best gown, the green one.'

'There's a stain on the skirt' she interrupted.

'Then sponge it off! Surely you've more to do than illspeak my father to me?'

If she had given me a pleading look I might've relented and even begged her pardon for my rudeness, but she shot me a sour glance and went out, leaving the study door to slam in the draught from the hall.

That evening I wore my green gown and we supped on goose and roast ham and the last of the summer's fruits in the study where my mother had once offered my father help with his reading.

Mr Heathcliff came down looking spruce and handsome in his usual dark clothes – usual when he came into Ireland I mean, for I had no idea how he dressed when he was in England.

We sat at the round table in the room where details of my

estate lay locked away in the desk once more and there were no ghosts there, only for the first time an easy companionship as he talked with good sense on a variety of subjects. He had travelled widely in his youth, even in the near East and he described cities domed with gold and narrow alleys where veiled women walked in slippered feet.

To this day I have no notion what was true and what invention. I only know that he entertained me and made me feel like a grown-up lady for the first time in my life.

On my instructions he had been put in one of the better bedrooms and I had ordered that a fire be lit there every evening. He seemed to take it as his due rather than a favour, and I wonder to this day if he spent more than an hour at a time sleeping, for long after midnight I looked out of my window and saw light coming from his chamber further along the wing.

Two or three nights after his arrival I resolved to ask him if all was to his liking and so rose, slipped on robe and slippers and went along the passage to tap at his door.

There was no answer from within but I heard footsteps from beyond the closed door and then the sound of the bolt being pulled free.

He stood in shirt and trousers on the threshold of the room and there was something wild and strained in his look as he stared at me. Then he said in a harsh whisper, 'Have you seen her? Has she followed me here?'

'Who?' I asked, though I knew well he wasn't speaking of my mother.

'Never mind!' He shook back his hair which had strayed from the confining ribbon and looked past my shoulder into the dark passage. In the room behind him every candle draped itself in a winding sheet and the fire blazed.

'I wished to ask if you were all right,' I said.

For answer he took my chin in his hand and went on gazing

at me hungrily. Yet his next words were prosaic enough.

'In the half-light you remind me of myself,' he said. 'Before the world became a wasteland and there was still hope in hell. Go to your bed, girl, and leave me to pass the night in my own fashion. I might be proud of you yet if you seek to please me. Good night, Aspen Stewart!'

'Good night,' I answered.

And I heard the pacing begin again the instant the door was shut, as if he resumed some interrupted happening that played itself out in his troubled mind.

In the morning I wrote out instructions for Mr Alistair, telling him to raise the rents of my tenants by a few pence, enough to show them that it was within my power to remit them altogether or reduce the cottagers to starvation, and I laid a copy on the table for Mr Heathcliff to peruse when he entered.

He read the instructions without remark and then leaned to kiss my cheek and push back my unbound hair.

'You begin to please me,' was all he said.

SEVEN

The rains dwindled as November advanced and a pale, watery sun struggled through the clouds to reveal meadows turned into swamps and trees leaning, untidy with the last of their falling leaves, to gaze at their own reflections in the brown streams.

Mr Heathcliff rode out one morning, giving no intimation when he might return, so I told the maids to keep his room aired and a fire going and found myself wandering through the other rooms, thinking how large and silent they seemed. In the end I put on boots and cloak and squelched over to Imdel, for, while a building may be lonely, a glen and a ruined fort impart something that stirs imagination and banishes solitude.

The fort was crumbling further into ruin, stone settling upon stone, fern and weed blurring the outlines. I stood and looked round me, half hoping to hear the Brunty girls playing somewhere near at hand but on this chill winter day they would be indoors by the fire and the lads at their work.

'Miss Aspen!'

It was Hugh Brunty, waving as he plodded towards me across the slopes, his features thinner and sharper than when I had seen him last.

'Mr Brunty! How tired you look!' was my first ill-judged remark for he frowned at it, then said with assumed heartiness,

'That's a sad greeting for a friend! I am better than I was a week ago when the cough held me in its grip! You look blooming!'

'I have had my father's company,' I said, raising my chin as if to beat down disapproval.

'Aye, so I heard. Was it he talked you into raising the rents of your tenants?'

'These are difficult days,' I said.

'For some more than others.'

'Have the Bruntons and the O'Malleys been grumbling to you?' I enquired.

'I met Mr Alistair who told me you had sent word,' he said. 'Though you don't hold all the rents or the shares until you are twenty-one you still have a large say in how affairs are conducted. He will do as you wish but he is not happy about it.'

'Mr Alistair now talks over my affairs with you, does he?' I said crossly.

'He does not, but he evidently feels strongly about this for he let it slip in conversation. Aspen, darling—'

'I will not show weakness by going back on my word,' I told him.

'Your grandfather would not have acted so,' Hugh Brunty said.

'Grandfather died and the estate is mine now. Why don't you look to your own affairs and leave me to manage mine?'

'I advised as a friend,' he said. 'So, you have had your father's company these past days. I trust he treats you kindly.'

'He begins to respect me,' I said.

'I am glad you did not say "love",' he said. 'To be loved by Mr Heathcliff must be as destructive as to be hated by him.'

'You first brought him here with the best of intentions!'

'An extra paving stone on the road to hell,' he said wryly. 'Miss Aspen, I have spoken out of turn today but Ellis and I have always been fond of you and of your grandfather who was good to me and mine in hard times and though it is none of our affair we have hoped to see you happy as we are happy.'

With ten children in a small house and the cough sapping his vigour day by day I thought.

Instead I asked, 'My mother, Rosina, was sweet natured and loving people say. Do you think she loved my father or did he. . . ?'

'I wasn't privy to their meetings,' he replied, 'but I would guess that he – he can be very charming when he pleases.'

'But he did not love her,' I said sadly.

'He is like me,' Hugh Brunty began.

'Hardly! You are flower and flint!'

'Myself being the flower I daresay?' He smiled at that, looking more his old self. 'We are alike in that we only love once and that love lasts beyond living and dying. In all other ways, no. Will you walk over to the church with me? I've a bunch of sweet rosemary to lay on your mother's tomb.'

On my rare visits there I had sometimes seen a posy and wondered who had placed it there, supposing that Brigit might've done so.

'You remember her with posies,' I said. 'That's kind of you.'

'Ellis generally reminds me. Where's Jackdaw?'

'In the stable, pain free but losing weight.'

'I'll walk over in a day or two and see what happens.'

We came to the church and he pushed open the heavy door. My grandfather and grandmother slept here now side by side but they were separated from my mother by a carved pillar and I recalled my childish fantasy that one day she would wake and find her stone coverlet too heavy to lift.

He laid the posy of herbs and blessed himself. I stood by, seeing the wooden pews were swollen with damp and there was dust on the aisle. It was, I thought, a long time since I had been to any service. As a small girl I had been taken regularly but of late I had scarcely troubled myself with worship, nor did this brief visit induce me to come more often to the services. If the dead returned they rode horseback and melted into mist.

'God rest her soul,' Hugh Brunty said. 'I'll walk home with you, Miss Aspen.'

'We shall not quarrel again I hope?'

'Was that a quarrel?' He shot me a quizzical glance from under his sandy brows. 'I have a habit of looking upon you as a kind of foster daughter, forgetting you are now the lady of the manor. If I spoke out of turn then I apologize.'

'No need. A little plain speaking never harmed anyone,' I assured him. 'However I don't promise to agree with your opinion.'

'Only mind a little what I say to you about Mr Heathcliff.' His look grew troubled again. 'There truly is something about him that is dark and devious. I didn't see it when he was a boy. It grew upon him like fungus on a rare plant or perhaps it was in him from the beginning, waiting to be stirred into life. Now what mishap?'

He spoke half in amusement, half in irritation as one of his daughters, Mary, came running down the glen.

'What's to do?' He took her hand and peered into her solemn little face.

'Our mammy says can you come because our James has been playing japes on the neighbours again,' she trilled breathlessly. 'He's been in the neighbourhood dressed up as a lady – a gypsy with a red shawl and all and been so clever that not one soul knew who it was, and he's taken money for telling fortunes and he isn't a fortune-teller at all!'

'He isn't a lady either,' Hugh Brunty said with a grin. 'Excuse us, Miss Aspen, while I go and sort my errant tribe out! I wonder if Moses had the same trouble!'

He laughed, swung Mary up into his arms and went off in the

direction of his house.

I wondered how it would be to form one of a large family with brothers and sisters to share, and there was often little enough to share when seasons were hard! And as I entered the main gates and walked up the drive I was glad that it was all mine and never to be divided with others or parcelled out among relatives.

I knew as soon as I entered the hall that my father had returned from whatever errand had taken him away for a few days. He stood by the fireplace in the study, turning the logs with the tip of his foot and his glance when he looked at me was replete with lazy amusement like a cat who has stolen the cream and sees another punished for it.

'You've been hobnobbing with the peasants again,' he said without heat. 'There's a bit of the peasant in you, maybe?'

'Not from my grandfather!' I said.

'And all the Bruntys claim kinship with the kings of Tara, I suppose?'

'James Brunty dressed up as a gypsy and went round telling fortunes.'

I pulled off my cloak and tossed it over a chair.

'Probably a bit of the Romany in them too,' he remarked.

'And in you?'

He gave that exasperating shrug with which he parried enquiry.

'Maybe so. My foster father told people that he picked me up when he went on a business trip to Liverpool. He did the round trip of one hundred and twenty miles on foot in three days and was exhausted when he returned.'

'He was a poor man?'

'One of the warmest in the district with a brace of fine horses in the stables.'

'Then why?'

'No idea! Not really interested. I recall nothing of the journey myself. It has always felt as if I were born at . . . the house where I was reared. What have you been doing?'

'Nothing much.'

'There speaks the lady of leisure! Well, my bit of business was concluded satisfactorily, so we may relax and enjoy each other for a spell.'

'Did you go to Dublin?' I asked.

'My affairs are my affairs.'

'I hoped,' I explained, 'that you might've brought me a present.'

'I gave you a present once and you no longer wear it.'

'You said it was very fragile so I keep it in a box. I can show you if you don't believe me.'

'Oh, I believe you,' he said. 'Only a fool would lie to me and you are no fool!'

'How long are you staying?' I asked.

'A day or two more and then I return into Yorkshire, and you may curb that triumphant smile for I was going to tell you anyway.'

'Yorkshire is in the north of England.'

'The West Riding to be more precise. I live out on the moors near the village of Gimmerton.'

'You have an estate?'

'A working farm but the house is large. Before too long I hope to be in possession of a more elegant property.'

'You are going to be married again?'

'My son will hopefully soon be wed. I told you before.'

'Linton,' I said thoughtfully.

'Aye!' His mouth twisted into a grimace. 'Linton, my son. His bride to be—'

'Your niece by marriage.'

'So you do retain some of my sayings? My niece is a pretty

94

little filly, spoilt and silly like most girls!'

'I am not like most girls!' I said.

'Indeed you are not!' He shot me a glance compounded of pride and chagrin. 'Anyway I have no present for you. You may wait for a handsome lover to festoon you with gifts!'

'I have no lover, handsome or otherwise,' I said. 'You spoke of another young man, a relative who lives in ignorance?'

'Aye, cousin to my son and the girl who will become my daughter-in-law. Ten times better than Linton!'

'Whom you mistreat?'

'To test his loyalty.' He gave a short, bitter laugh. 'He has grown to manhood believing me to be his staff and shield against the world. And I may yet become his benefactor if all my fruits ripen at the same time! If you wish to please me—'

'I wish first to please myself,' I said.

'And so you shall, provided it chimes with my own desires. Now call that witch Brigit and tell her I will be staying for a few days more. She'll not know whether to thank God kneeling that I contemplate departure or beseech the Almighty to bear me off to hell before the night's out!'

I went into the kitchen to call Brigit and saw from the scowl on her face that she had already divined his intent.

'Mother of God,' she mumbled, 'but we've to endure his presence for longer! Why must he visit at all? For sure your grandfather, God rest his soul, would not have welcomed him.'

'I am not my grandfather,' I told her plainly. 'I am myself alone and it gives me pleasure to know that I have one relative who looks out for my welfare.'

'Keeps an eye on your estate you mean,' she said. 'And don't be thinking you fool me, Miss Aspen, with your talk of loving relatives. It's my belief you half envy him his sneaking ways – like a fox in a hen coop! But take good heed that you are not the hen!'

I left her to her complaining and went back to the study but Mr Heathcliff had evidently gone upstairs to wash and change for the rest of the day.

He was always, though plainly dressed, neat and clean in his appearance though his dark features and black eyes gave him at all times the look of a gypsy.

He had left his bag on a chair in the corner, unhasped and ready for the inquisitive hand. I went over and opened it carefully, seeing a sheaf of papers on top. The papers seemed to register various transactions argued over in Dublin and Liverpool. There was also a list of shipping times to China and the near East and some rough paper on which figures were scrawled apparently at random.

Nothing in the documents meant anything to me save that my father traded in far-flung places. The bottom of the bag held only a pair of shoes and a woollen muffler. I repacked everything in order, taking care to leave the bag half open and went up to my own room to change my attire.

I had just secured my hair in a green ribbon to match my dress when I heard a sound, muffled yet loud, issuing from the other side of the building. I paused, fingers still trapped in the ribbon bow, and then resumed my toilet, added a dash of perfume and went downstairs.

'Oh, Miss Aspen!'

One of the servants, a rather silly girl who was employed mainly to do the rough work, came towards me along the passage. Her face was tearstreaked and her hands were wringing the folds of her apron.

'Molly, what ails you?' I demanded.

Her round face quivered as she pointed down the passage. She muttered something that I failed to catch and fled past me, still sobbing loudly.

'Mr Heathcliff.'

I spoke his name under my breath as I hurried past her to where a door gave entry to the stableyard.

And I knew even as I entered what had brought forth her woe. Jackdaw's stall was open and Mr Heathcliff stood, looking down at the gun still smoking in his hand.

Jackdaw lay within the stall, legs collapsed beneath her and a thick trickle of blood issuing from one nostril. There was no sound save the faint keening of the breeze in the yard and an occasional snicker from one of the other horses lodged nearby.

'I'll have someone take the carcass away,' Mr Heathcliff said.

'Hugh Brunty said that he would—'

'Get Brunty to shoot one of the other horses if you've promised him a killing,' Mr Heathcliff said. 'The wretched beast was slowly starving to death and you were delaying the end as if you were Lord God Almighty.'

'I wanted to say goodbye,' I heard myself say.

'You think the poor beast noticed your loving absence? Now do not give way to tears for the sake of everything sacred and profane! You have money enough to buy yourself a dozen horses more and ride them to death on alternative Saturdays! I shall be in to take a glass of wine with you in a few minutes or you may indulge in a spot of brandy if you wish.'

He spoke calmly, coldly, brutally even as he knelt and stroked the unbreathing satiny hide with a gentle hand.

I choked back my tears out of pride for I had no intention of letting Mr Heathcliff see my weakness, a quality I was already well aware he despised and would turn to his own advantage. Instead I held my head high and said, 'You are right. A pony is only a beast after all. You may drink the brandy yourself if you've a mind.'

I went back into the house, rated Molly soundly for making a fool of herself and gave orders for the removal of the carcass and then I went into the study and carefully measured out a glass of wine and drank it in two or three gulps.

'Good God! the girl's a toper already!' Mr Heathcliff cried as he entered. 'You would have had stiff competition from my late foster brother in the art of drinking oneself senseless! Ah! you have no doubt examined the contents of my bag thoroughly? If not then you shall not have a second opportunity.'

'I understood none of it,' I said.

'One day I shall explain the business dealings I have and teach you lessons never learnt in a schoolroom,' he said. 'Pour me that tot of brandy, will you?'

I poured it, hating him with every nerve and sinew and stood as he drank it down.

'This is for you!' He took a piece of forelock from his pocket and put it on the table.

I picked it up, feeling Jackdaw beneath me once more as we rode along the glen, hearing her welcoming whinny when I came.

'Don't fret, daughter,' Mr Heathcliff said, and his hand pulled not ungently at my own hair. 'Eat your supper, sleep well and all shall be right in the morning.'

EIGHT

At breakfast Mr Heathcliff said to me, 'I've business further afield this morning. I'd be glad if you went down into the village to make a couple of purchases for me.'

'If you wish,' I said, glancing up to meet his ironic gaze.

'A leather purse if the saddler has one such and a silk shawl.'

'The purse can be readily obtained but I doubt if you'll find a silk shawl in the village,' I said.

'Then the finest wool,' he stipulated.

'And they are for . . .'

'The Bruntys,' he said to my complete astonishment. 'I owe Hugh Brunty a kind of debt for it was he who brought me here and his wife is still a pretty woman. I like to pay my debts in full, sooner or later.'

'They may not take gifts from you,' I protested. 'Hugh Brunty regrets the day he brought you into Imdel.'

'Say they are from you for past kindnesses then. Your stock will rise and I care not a jot for my standing! There's money enough here, I think?'

He scattered coins over the table and rose.

'I'll do it then,' I said. 'It wouldn't suit me to have your own reputation improved.'

He merely grinned at that and went out into the hall where

he paused for a moment before mounting the stairs.

I walked down to the village, having no desire to ride that morning, and purchased the items he wanted. I chose the handsomer of two leather purses and, since my foreboding that silk would not be available proved true, a beautiful shawl of the finest white wool for Ellis.

There were coins left over and I put them in the purse before ordering the gifts to be wrapped and then, feeling slightly lighter of heart, made my way to the Brunty house.

A dank chill hung over the building and the edges of the thatch were dark from the recent rain. I could see the glint of a fire through the windows so went up and tapped at the door.

'Miss Aspen, this is a welcome surprise!' Ellis said, letting me into the warm bright living-room. 'Look who's come calling, Hugh!'

'Are you well both of you?'

I addressed the question more to him than her for she looked blooming whereas he seemed greyer and thinner suddenly as if youth was taking a last farewell.

'The cough's easing, thank you,' he said, rising to greet me, his handclasp as firm as ever.

'Jackdaw passed away,' I said.

'Well, we knew it was coming. Poor old girl!' He looked at me with sympathy. 'She had a long life and a pleasant one. I hope her end was swift? I've been expecting you to ask me to—'

'Mr Heathcliff shot her.'

'Then I hope he didn't take too much pleasure in the pulling of the trigger,' he said.

'One shot through the head. She was right off her feed anyway,' I felt obliged to add.

'How long is Mr Heathcliff staying?' Ellis asked, bringing over a pot of tea and some cake.

'Another two or three days and then he returns into the north of England. Oh, I took the liberty of bringing you both something.' I handed over the packages.

'For us? Why, Miss Aspen?' Hugh asked.

'Against past kindnesses,' I said lightly. 'I hope you won't hurt my feelings by refusing?'

'It's little enough we've ever done,' Ellis said, untying her parcel and shaking out the folds of the shawl. 'Oh, now this is pretty! I've been promising myself for ages that I will knit myself a new Sunday shawl but with the lads going through their stockings as fast as dogs coursing hares, I never seem to get a moment!'

Hugh, looking at the leather purse, said more quietly, 'This is good of you, Miss Aspen darling! We've been trying to put a bit by to help the family when it's needed, and – well, I thank you kindly for it.'

'So what news of the family?' I enquired.

'All well though Janie catches cold too easily, but the other girls are growing up fast.'

'Though they're never going to be as beautiful as their mother,' Hugh put in.

'Listen to the man!' She flicked the shawl towards him playfully. 'Pat's doing well, saving to go to the university in England, but William is still talking about a united Ireland. We're hoping his lady friend will sweep such notions out of his head. Hughie and James are looking for some road mending jobs before the winter settles in and Welsh is helping out any way he can. It seems to me they all grow up so fast. You look at them toddling round your knees, and look away and when you look back they are grown up with minds of their own.'

'It must be a great worry having such a large family,' I said, ignoring the odd sensation of a lonely little space having opened up inside me somewhere.

'And a great deal of laughter,' she said.

'Have you made plans for Christmas yet?' Hugh asked. 'We were hoping you'd come by and share some of the *craic* with us maybe?'

'I shall probably look in.' I finished the tea and rose.

'It's been a real pleasure,' Hugh said, also rising.

'About that cough . . .' I hesitated. 'I can send some medicine that may ease it.'

'God save us, Miss Aspen, but you've done enough!' Hugh opened the door for me as I adjusted my cloak. 'With these coins I can buy my own cough medicine! Anyway it eases when the warmer weather arrives.'

'And I'll not keep you from your fireside,' I said, seeing he was set to walk with me. 'Good day, Ellis. God bless all here!'

I walked home, irritated to find that the mud in the lanes had crept over the tops of my boots and stained my stockings. Not that it mattered since I had shoes and stockings enough to supply the whole Brunty family.

Mr Heathcliff was nowhere to be seen. Ridden to Dublin, I supposed and dismissed him from my mind.

The midday meal I took alone and afterwards, feeling restless and ill at ease, went round to the stables. By now Jackdaw would have been carted away but her stall with its water bucket and feeding trough would still be there. For an instant I almost turned back and then I told myself not to be a fool and went past the other stalls to where I had last seen my pony lying with blood trickling slowly from one nostril.

There was no carcass and no straw, no water bucket nor feeding trough, only the scrubbed stone floor. Even her saddle had gone from its place and her currycomb no longer hung on the wall.

'Mr Heathcliff ordered it all done, Miss Aspen,' Brigit informed me as I stood staring.

She had followed me down the passage and stood, breathing

rapidly in the chilly air.

'You take his orders now, do you?' I said.

'It seemed best you not being here,' she explained. 'And he said that it was hard to come into a place where death had visited and find memories waiting there. Anyway he had it done.'

'You take your orders from me in future,' I scolded.

'Yes, Miss Aspen, but he's always had a way of giving commands that makes you wonder what he'd do if you refused him,' she said.

'We must try it some time and find out.' I said drily, pushing past her out of the stables.

'Miss Aspen!' She followed me, her voice lower and less strident. 'Miss Aspen!'

'What is it?' Coming into the side hall I stopped and turned to face her.

'Miss Aspen, I know you're nineteen now and a grown lady,' she said, 'and the days when I could scold you are long past but there's something I need to say even if I'm dismissed for it.'

'Something unpleasant no doubt?'

'Miss Aspen, I was nurse to your mother, God rest her sweet soul, when I was just a young woman myself, and since I never wed I looked on her as my child in a manner of speaking,' she said in a rush. 'She was the sweetest little colleen you can imagine, with her pretty red hair and her winning ways. And then Hugh Brunty brought that sullen, dark gypsy lad here and took a fancy to him though I shall never be able to figure out why, for though he worked hard there was something about him that made me bless myself when he went by. And then the master began to favour him and bring him up in the ways of business and buying and selling and after that Hugh Brunty might count himself fortunate if he got a nod in passing! And then Miss Rosina began to look at him—'

'He's a handsome man still,' I broke in.

'Aye, and can charm anything he pleases when he wishes. My Miss Rosina took a great liking to him and helped him with his reading and writing and persuaded her father to have him sit at meals with them and ape the manners of his betters. And one time as I was coming from mass I saw them in the orchard. He was pushing the swing and she was laughing with her hair blowing out in the wind and her skirts flying up. And I saw his face as he pushed the swing! It was white and set and there was something in it made me bless myself and hurry past. And then the master sent for me and told me they were going to Dublin for a week or two. I asked Miss Rosina why but she wouldn't answer me. And they went along with Mr Alistair and when she came back she had a wedding-ring on and we were all told to call Heathcliff, Mr Heathcliff from then on. And though she always greeted him very lovingly when he returned from one of the master's business trips I never heard them laughing together, never saw him put an arm round her. He's a wicked man, Miss Aspen, and the master rued the day he'd trusted him just as Hugh Brunty rued having brought him here in the first place.'

She had put her hand on my arm and I shook it off impatiently.

'And you fear that I might admire him?' I said. 'Not so! I know he has great charm when he wishes to use it and a filthy temper and that my grandfather must have had good reason for cutting him out of his will, but I am not like my mother to be bedazzled by honey words.'

'No, indeed you are not, Miss Aspen,' she said. 'You have only the tinge of red in your hair and your pretty laugh to remind me of her, but you have his dark eyes and every time he comes here I see more of him in you – the way you hold your head, the way you take longer strides and raise your voice when you give orders to the maids.'

'He begat me and has some share in me,' I said. 'And there is some feeling in him I believe. No human being is entirely a devil.'

'And who said he was ever a human being?' she retorted and went past me as fast as her legs could move.

I went on upstairs and looked into the pierglass on my bedroom wall, sought traces of a sweet red-haired girl, and saw my father looking out of my eyes, saw my lip curl slightly as I had seen his curl. And beating back a sudden unmentionable terror, I laughed in triumph at my own shadow self and fancied I heard an answering peal of mockery that came from nowhere but began and ended inside my own head.

Mr Heathcliff returned late the next day, interrupting me as I sat at my supper.

'No, I'm not hungry!' He spoke impatiently as I indicated the place set ready for him.

'Take a glass of wine then,' I said. 'You must be tired after your long ride.'

If I'd imagined that would have brought forth some account of where he'd been I would have been disappointed. He merely smiled slightly and poured himself a modest ration, slung his cloak over the back of a chair and sat down at the far end of the table, tapping his fingers on the side of his glass in an irregular tattoo.

'It was thoughtful of you,' I said hesitatingly, 'to have Jackdaw taken away and the stall cleaned while I was in the village.'

'The carcass would've stank otherwise,' he said. 'You saw the Bruntys?'

'They were very pleased with my gifts.'

'Your gifts, of course!' He sent me an ironic glance.

'You said you would be returning into Yorkshire soon.'

'Aye, tomorrow, so there's no need to send barbed hints in my direction,' he said. 'My business is more or less wound up here and I go home a far richer man. Knowing we share a fondness for money you will be pleased at that information, I daresay?'

'Naturally,' I said. 'You and I both like to have money. Indeed I venture to say that the love of money is our overriding concession to feelings.'

'For God's sake, who spoke of feelings?' he barked suddenly. 'You have no notion what having feelings is like! A tame affection for your grandfather's memory and a Lady Bountiful bending to a few people in the village is the nearest you've ever come to feeling anything! Passion and love, love that eats you alive, are foreign words to you!'

'I am but nineteen,' I reminded him.

'So was she,' he said, so quietly that I strained to catch the words. 'Nineteen when she died, and in her nineteen years she had known and inflicted more passionate tenderness and more selfish cruelty than you or a thousand others will know in a long lifetime!'

'And she was beautiful,' I said quietly.

'Was she?' He seemed to ponder his own query for a moment. 'She was, I suppose, beautiful. When I looked at her my soul dissolved in the contemplation of my own inner being. When she was led astray by her own greed for position and wealth then my likeness was shattered like cracked ice on a millpond. Until I knew her I had no sense of myself and after she rejected me I built a new self in the empty space where myself had dwelt. And when she died myself died too though my animal functions go on.'

'She died a long time ago,' I said, seeking to heal some hurt beyond any hurt I could understand.

'All the years since have become one year and all the days one day,' he said vehemently. 'She died yesterday and she is dying today and when I wake up tomorrow her dying will begin again. Others are shadows, filled with a semblance of life. And she is forever dying but never dead for she follows me. She lurks in corners, raises her voice when the church bells chime, peers at me from every crevice, blows down the back of my neck when I sit alone, whisks round corners before I can turn and catch a glimpse of her skirt. I never see her but she is always there. And you think you know what loving is!'

I thought of the shadow shape I had glimpsed and found a long shudder coursing the marrow of my bones.

'She feeds on you,' I said uneasily.

'Exactly!' He thumped his fist so hard on the table as he rose that I winced in sympathy. 'She drinks my heart's blood and is never satisfied! And she never gives me sight of even the tip of her little finger.'

'My mother loved you I think,' I said.

'Rosina was a sweetly pretty creature with a large inheritance,' he said more quietly. 'I found her attractive bait and she had a romantic fondness for me. She tried to ease a gaping wound with an embroidered handkerchief. We saw little of each other after the wedding.'

'And your second wife? Linton's mother?'

'A sleek little kitten until you offended her feelings, which I took pleasure in doing a hundred times a day, and then she turned into a spitting alley-cat. She ran away and kept her son from me until her death, but if I'd crooked my little finger she'd've come running for more punishment! When she suffered she knew she was alive and it gave her pleasure to taunt and tease until I struck out.'

'Poor Linton!' I could not help exclaiming.

'Spoilt, idle, delicate, selfish and petulant,' he answered. 'He and my niece will make a fine pair of lovebirds between them.'

'And the other nephew, the one you deprived of education or status?'

'Oh, I have plans to better him beyond his dreams sooner or

107

later,' he said. 'Is that the time? The hour's later than I thought. I'll bid you good-night until the morning. I ride by way of Imdel Fort just after dawn. Will you come with me as far as that?'

'You killed my pony,' I said.

'I'll have one of the other horses saddled up for you. Good night!'

He had left the room before I could reply and I heard his slow tread upon the stairs as if he feared mounting them, feared the shape that held his soul and hovered out of sight and touch.

I poured myself another glass of wine, steadying one hand with the other and wished he had never returned even though pity, like slow spirals of fire, twisted my nerves.

When I finally went upstairs his door was closed. Driven by some impulse I tapped gently and, trying the handle, found it unlocked.

There were no candles lit and he sat on the windowseat, gazing through the open casement. Beyond, the moon was rising higher, bright and shining, to contradict November. As I stepped closer I saw black drops falling like rain from his wrist where he had inflicted a dozen small cuts with a sharp paperknife he held in his other hand.

'She never visited Ireland,' he said, aware of my entering though he never turned his head. 'If she ventures forth tonight I'd not have her lose her way.'

I stood there, watching him, not moving, until I too began to feel like a ghost moving through someone else's life and then I left the room and went to my own, locking the door and stirring up the fires and setting lighted candles in every sconce and huddled in my dressing-gown until the moon sank and the candles guttered in their sockets and the logs in the fireplace turned into smouldering red ash that blackened as the dawn came, and I could not tell if I had failed or not at some task I ought, as a daughter, to have performed.

When I went downstairs I was heavy eyed, the green of my riding-habit imparting a sallow tinge to my skin. Mr Heathcliff stood by the table in the dining-room, hastily finishing some breakfast. He cast me an incurious look as I sat down and poured myself some tea.

'You'll have to make haste,' he remarked. 'When I say that I'll leave at first light I mean at first light. I've ordered the horses saddled.'

It wasn't his place to order anything but I let the matter slide past and hastily drank my tea and wolfed a scone.

Brigit, hands folded over her apron, stood by the door, looking grim and saying nothing. Her eyes were on Mr Heathcliff as avidly as if she feared he might hide the teaspoons and she merely grunted in reply to my muttered good-morning.

'Let's be off then,' he said curtly and went out into the hall.

'Where are you going?' Brigit demanded in a furious whisper. 'Mother of God, but he might force you over to England!'

'Don't be foolish!' I said sharply.

'Who knows what's in that one's mind?' she responded. 'You take care now, Miss Aspen.'

I left her to her grumbling and went to get my cloak. One of the other horses waited by the mounting block and as I gathered up the reins, Mr Heathcliff trotted round the corner on the black horse he always rode when he visited, though whether it had always been the same animal over the years was impossible to tell.

'We'll ride to the fort,' he said.

'Is there some particular reason?'

'A whim.' He spoke lightly but I doubted if whims ever moved him.

It was cool and damp after the previous day, with a blurred sky and languid sun. Under the horses' hooves the glen was springy and the grass greener than in a dry winter.

'This country of yours will sap my energies,' he said as we rode up towards the fort. 'It's a land for bards and lovers not granite-hearted businessmen.'

'Yorkshire is more bracing I suppose?' I said.

'Aye! Very bracing at times. It puts spirit in a person. When you're herding sheep in a full force gale you've little time to invent poems. Get down.'

As he dismounted and turned away to tether his horse to the bare branch of a thorn bush I found myself wondering about the place where he lived. Had it formed him after the age of seven or had other more potent influences marked his character?

'Your mother lies in the church yonder,' he said.

'You came here to visit her?' I said, confused.

'Visiting the living is labour enough without having to shake hands with the dead,' he said, amused.

'I don't visit often enough myself,' I confessed.

'Why should you? You never knew her.'

I wondered where his long lost Cathy was laid and if he ever went there.

He said, startling me by the aptness of his remark to my unspoken question, 'There is one grave I haunt and will do so until I die. Not that her essence lies there – her essence haunts me and I haunt her bones. That's the irony of it! We likely pass each other along the way.'

'She never showing herself,' I said.

'Not the gleam of a fingernail or the tip of a shoe,' he said, seating himself on one of the large stones about the half-ruined building. 'She is always behind me or just around the bend in the road. I could make whirlwinds by turning rapidly to find her, to catch one glimpse of her. We were two bound together against the world and she chose the world. She sat beneath a green sapling of an apple tree and rejected the oak that would have saved her from herself. And the question that twists and turns in my mind is "why"? Why did she throw everything aside for the sake of a summer fancy? Why was she not true? And why does she follow me now when I cannot see her or hold her or smell the clean, wild scent of her hair? There are times when I would welcome madness to be free of her and yet even in madness I would still crave the flitting of her shadow against the wall.'

'Perhaps you are not well?' I said cautiously.

'My problem,' he said, shrugging his shoulders as if to dislodge a weight, 'is that apart from a bout of measles I had as a child, I am one of the healthiest men I know. I am near forty and have the energy and endurance of two men of twenty years. And my mind is as sharp and clear as the mind of any ambitious, self-made man. Your grandfather recognized that and trusted me with his business affairs. He'd've done better to keep a sharp eye on his daughter!'

'As you do on me?' I said, and did not even try to disguise the sarcasm in my tone.

I had instinctively moved to a little distance away as I spoke, knowing as I did how his temper could flash in an instant.

He merely gave a weary sigh and rested his head in his hands for a moment. When he looked up again his voice was quiet, almost gentle.

'If I had not other plans ready to come to fruition,' he said, 'I would effect a particular punishment for your undaughterliness. But my mood is focused on the triumph of my wishes and later when that goal is attained I will turn my attention to you.'

'How can I be anything other when you visit so seldom and tell me so little?' I said.

'I've told you more than I've told many.' His brooding gaze was fixed upon me again. 'God help you if they turn up as tales in Hugh Brunty's repertoire!'

'I know when to keep silent,' I said.

'Then keep silent about this! I've a mate picked out for you whom I'm convinced you will love. As he will love you, for I've moulded him to do my bidding without question. And I owe the lad something for all the bad treatment I suffered from his father.'

'The downtrodden serf?'

'Aye, it shall be in your power to raise him. You will do so because he's a handsome animal, fit for breeding, and I've a mind to found a dynasty. When you think about it, Adam never knew his parentage either!'

He had spoken of madness and as he crouched on the stone, one hand caressing his injured wrist, his eyes ablaze with some dark, lambent fire, I began to wonder if he was already insane.

Then he said briskly in his usual tone, 'In two years you will attain control of your estate. You will be twenty-one. I shall not come into Ireland again but you may visit me.'

'In Yorkshire? Where do you—'

'Go to Gimmerton and take a room at the inn there,' he said. 'Either you will find my dwelling or I will find you.'

'And if I don't come?'

'You will come. Your curiosity will float you across the Irish Sea,' he said. 'Time I was riding! Oh, I bought these for you in Dublin! Who knows but they may solve the answer to a riddle that has defeated even me. Open them when I'm gone.'

Indeed he had half risen to leave but sank down again upon the stone, not moving but quivering in every limb, his head raised as if he sought something just out of sight. So searching was his regard that I turned my own head instinctively but saw only the horses grazing on the turf that lay between the stones, great clods of earth upturned by the recent rains, worms writhing in the dark soil.

His gaze shifted abruptly to the window spaces in the old fort where cobwebs did duty for curtains and rampant ivy sucked at the stones.

'I thought I saw a shadow,' he said, shaking his head as if to empty it of imagination. 'Even here where she never came she still hides from me. We used to play hide and seek among the tombstones when we were mere children. She always hid and I always followed her trail: a bow of ribbon, a torn page from an exercise book, her laughter lingering on the air, and she always leapt out from the place where I had last looked and we kissed there among the mouldering graves that shawled the bones of those who might have risen up in joy at the sound of our voices.'

'Cathy,' I said, and felt a tenderness melt my flesh.

'She was me and I was her,' he said musingly. 'I wish – Aspen, do you know what I wish for at this moment if she will not come?'

'No,' I said.

'I wish someone would just hold me,' he said, and his voice quivered in a manner that shredded the years.

I stood motionless, gripping the little box he had tossed to me, wanting to move, unable to move.

I heard a long sigh issuing from him and then he rose, went to where the horses grazed, untethered his black stallion, and mounted up.

'Gimmerton when you are twenty-one!' he said, not turning to look at me. 'Seek me there!'

He dug his spurs in sharply and the horse leaped forward. Mr Heathcliff made no motion of farewell but I saw for a fleeting instant the outline of the woman who sat behind him and heard far off the faint tinkling of either laughter or bells.

I sat down and opened the box carefully. Under its lid, nestling against velvet, were earrings shaped like little scarlet apples, and I remembered what he had once told me about the figure from his lost childhood who had worn tiny apples in her plaits.

I thought then, as I think now, they were the saddest things I had ever seen.

NINE

'And will you visit him, Miss Aspen?' Hugh Brunty asked.

'I am of full age in two months,' I told him, 'and I shall take ship for Liverpool and then travel up into Yorkshire to seek him out.'

'They say Yorkshire's a big county,' he said doubtfully.

'I have the name of a village where I shall stay. He has set me the task of finding him and I have accepted the challenge,' I said airily.

'Then I hope he hasn't moved house', Hugh Brunty said. 'I'd put nothing past that one.'

'Mr Brunty!' I turned to him impulsively. 'You must not regret bringing him to my grandfather's house for had you not I'd never have been born.'

'I've an inkling you'd've got yourself born sooner or later, somehow or other whether he'd come here or not,' Hugh Brunty said.

'Well, don't fret about the past,' I said.

'Actually I seldom do!' He gave a chuckle. 'What's done is done and the future is worrying enough if you're the worrying kind, which I am not!'

We were walking towards the glen and I paused to look out

over the fields of corn and potatoes that were almost ready for the harvesting.

'I shall miss this view,' I said.

'You're not planning on staying among the heathen English for ever surely?' he protested.

'Not for ever, no.'

I had a sudden absurd vision of myself arriving and of Mr Heathcliff welcoming me with the glad cry, 'Here is my darling daughter!'

The vision was so manifestly absurd and Mr Heathcliff so unlikely to behave in such a fashion that I wanted to laugh.

'I'd like to ask a favour, Miss Aspen,' Hugh Brunty said. 'It's about our Patrick actually.'

'He's in England now, isn't he?' I said, not much interested but polite.

'Starting at Cambridge University,' he said proudly. 'When I think that I once apprenticed him to a weaver! He'll be a great man one day, Miss Aspen. We always knew our Pat would get on!'

'And you were right,' I said warmly, and thought privately that Pat Brunty might still be teaching in a little local school had I not paid him out for the snub that had so wounded me when I was a child.

'His mother has knitted a couple of thick scarves against the English winter,' Hugh Brunty said, 'but it is a long way to send a parcel and he'd have to pay the postage the other end. If you could possibly put them in your luggage and then if your route lies anywhere near where he is—'

'I shall be travelling light,' I said, hastily adding as I saw the disappointment dawn in his pleasant face, 'so I will have room for a parcel.'

'That's good of you, Miss Aspen.' He wrung my hand warmly.

'I've a favour to ask in return,' I said. 'Brigit is getting on in years and though she won't admit it, her breathing is sometimes ragged and her ankles swell. If you were to visit her now and then, just to take heed of her progress. . . ?'

'And without her guessing my intent, eh? With pleasure, Miss Aspen. Favours exchanged between friends are the best favours I think.'

'And we are friends, are we not, Mr Brunty?'

Suddenly it seemed important that when I went into England there would be someone left in Ireland whom I could call a friend.

'Aye, in spite of the difference in our stations,' he said with a grin.

'In Ireland who troubles about that!' I exclaimed.

'More people than you'd guess, Aspen darling,' he said, putting an arm about my shoulders. 'Your grandfather, God rest his soul, treated all with the same fairness but in England they say there's a great gulf fixed between master and man.'

'I'll tell you all about it when I return,' I promised.

'And God speed you back to us,' he said quietly. 'I'm not much of a one for praying but it's troubled me sorely to see you so alone over the years. In England you might make friends – even find a mate!'

'I believe my father has one in mind for me,' I confided. 'Some adopted relative of his whom he has degraded to the level of a yokel and now plans to raise up a little. But I'll marry where I please!'

'Marry where you love,' he said, keeping his arm about me as we walked along. 'Marry where you love without limit, Miss Aspen.'

'I mean to,' I said. 'Oh, my God, what's that?'

I might well exclaim in fright for the dull booming that grated on the ear and rose to a wail before it sank into silence might have caused the banshee to flee.

Hugh Brunty burst out laughing.

'The girls found an old buffalo horn half buried down by the spring,' he said. 'With the boys working on the land and the roads and not one having a timepiece to bless himself with, and Ellis getting into a fret if we don't all sit down to supper together, the buffalo horn serves well as a clarion call. You'll eat with us this eve?'

'There will be too many,' I said.

'Pat's away and Will's gone further south to carry on his courting and Welsh is over working at the counting-house three nights a week, so there's room to spare,' he answered.

'Then I will, for soon I shall have little time for visiting with so much to arrange,' I said.

'You have escort to Dublin?'

'Mr Alistair will see me on to the boat. He does not approve of my travelling alone to England but when I informed him it was Mr Heathcliff's wish that I visit him he held his tongue. He will look after the affairs of the estate here until I return. I have left instructions regarding the buying-in of stock and seed for next year and the rent—'

'You're not going to raise them again?'

'No, so you may smile at me and postpone that frown,' I said as the last wailing of the horn echoed from the surrounding hills.

Already I could see them coming, the girls breaking into an impromptu dance, whirling over the grass with little bobbing steps, their fair curls bouncing on their shoulders and their arms held stiffly at their sides in traditional fashion while their brothers ran over the hill, tall Hughie already in the lead with James close behind.

And then Ellis emerged from the house, and ran to join us, waving to her children but having eyes only for her husband whom she embraced as fervently as if they had been parted for a year instead of an hour.

'Miss Aspen, you'll stay for supper?' she cried. 'We've space and to spare today and I've made colcannon.'

'Until you've tasted colcannon made by Ellis you've tasted nothing worth the swallowing!' Hugh Brunty said.

'Will you listen to the man now?' she pleaded. 'Sets me up as an expert and dooms a guest to disappointment! Did you ask. . . ?'

'I shall be glad to take the parcel for Pat,' I said. 'At least I can guarantee it will reach England though I cannot vouch for its safe arrival in Cambridge for I don't think my journey lies in that direction.'

'When it gets to England it will be in God's hands,' she said. 'Do you mark how the girls are growing, Miss Aspen? Surely we'll have to put bricks on their heads!'

Hughie had stopped to pull out a battered flute on which he began to play and Ellis joined her daughters, kicking, leaping and twirling with the same rapid grace while Hughie played his flute and James sat on the wall and beat time with his hands, and Hugh Brunty pressed my shoulder with his hand.

'Ellis is pleased that you'll take the parcel,' he said. 'She was shy about asking you but I said, "Miss Aspen is a friend and she'll carry out a small errand for love of you alone." She frets about Pat for he's always been apt to get colds in the winter.'

I watched them stream into the house, bulging its walls with their laughter and music and tapping feet and thought of the great house where I had grown up alone with only servants for company and the too-soon deaths of my mother and my dear grandfather to empty my world.

After supper she proudly showed me the scarves and wrapped them lovingly.

I put the parcel in my luggage and took it with me on the boat. I cannot tell if Pat Brunty ever laid eyes on them for when after a calm crossing we arrived at Liverpool with its bustling docks, huge warehouses and press of people of every colour, speaking a dozen different tongues, I lightened my luggage and tossed the parcel to a beggar who sat on the kerbside with his bare, filthy feet in the gutter.

TEN

I closed the journal in which a few brief entries summoned all my memories to revive and went over to the bench on which my travelling cases rested. I had brought the little box with the ring of bones and the box in which the little ruby apples lay. Now I changed my dress for a gown of light grey with a red sash and clipped the earrings into place and put on my cloak and went out downstairs into the taproom where a servant drawing ale merely nodded in the rough way of the locals as I passed and went into the street.

The previous night, the mists had lifted and the sky was a pale azure, blank and featureless, like the eyes of murdered children. In the street, villagers were going about their business and from the graveyard issued the inevitable sound of steel chipping stone.

I walked into the lane and reached the gate in the wall. When I looked through the bars I could see the little lawn before the house with a tangle of blackcurrant bushes filling one border and two young women who sat with writing-desks open on their knees and scribbled in pencil, not raising their heads as I paused to watch them.

One of them was the girl who had called for Keeper and sat on the stone above the water writing. She wrote now in what looked like haste, left hand moving rapidly across the paper. Her hair was dark with a coppery sheen, pulled back untidily into a Spanish comb and she wore a purple frock with flashes of white like lightning on it.

The other girl was slighter with fair hair curling to her neck and a dress of a darker grey than mine. Against her companion she was a pencil sketch against a painting.

'Miss – Stewart, isn't it?'

The Reverend Charnock came along the path to the gate.

'Good morning,' I said.

'Not seeing more imaginary young ladies I hope?' he said, in a would-be jocular tone.

'Mr Charnock, if you look to your right,' I said, annoyed at his manner, 'you will see . . . nothing.'

I ended on a dying fall for as I looked again to my own left I saw only the untidy square of grass with no sign of the young women or of the folding stools upon which they had been sitting.

'I agree,' he said somewhat drily.

'Mr Charnock, do you believe in ghosts?' I demanded.

'I believe the dead rest in peace save for those who have led evil lives and are trapped in another place,' he returned.

'A very comforting viewpoint,' I nodded and went on along the lane, thinking of the undead and of the yet to be born who must surely throng our world both in and out of dwelling places.

The stile climbed and a few small fields traversed, I came into the folds and billows of the open moor with its few scattered houses and great swathes of brown where the last of the heather had wilted.

I walked steadily, drawn by some instinct beyond myself, and saw the black crags rising before me and the ground dipping towards the shallow valley in which the Grange was set. Over to my left I saw again, as I had seen before, the large house set on the plateau above a rise with its narrow mullions and its barred gate.

I walked more slowly towards it, my shoes slipping now and then on the dew-damp moss that jewelled the grass and so arrived at the gate and saw beyond it a courtyard with stables and sheds set about the house and a bit of garden where someone had planted a few autumn-blooming flowers.

Mr Heathcliff was at home. I knew that even before I looked up and saw him standing at a window, its casement flapping in the breeze, one hand raised to beckon me, the other grasping the waist of someone who stood in the deep shadows behind him.

I lifted my own hand in greeting and leaned to unbar the gate. For a moment I stood uncertainly in the yard, expecting the front door to be opened at any moment and meanwhile amusing myself by looking at the carved stone gargoyles that surrounded its portals, small boys in a lamentable state of priapic nakedness frolicking about the name Hareton Earnshaw set in the midst with the date 1500.

The door opened suddenly to reveal a rather stout, pleasant-faced woman in a stuff gown with her hair neatly plaited at the back of her head.

'I saw you standing on the steps, miss,' she said in an accent that sounded more intelligible than others I had previously heard in this part of the country. 'Can I be of any help?'

I hesitated slightly before I replied, judging that Mr Heathcliff would want to make my identity known in his own way and not have it blurted out on his doorstep.

As I hesitated I saw her expression alter, a look almost of terror passing over her face before she shook her head slightly as if her gaze was blurred.

'My name is Aspen Stewart,' I said quickly. 'Is this Mr Heathcliff's property?'

'It was, miss. It belongs to Mrs Heathcliff now,' she said.

My father had taken another wife then? I reminded myself that in the almost two years since he had last visited me much might have happened.

'My grandfather had business dealings with Mr Heathcliff,' I said. 'I am here to – what is the name of this dwelling? I have been over to Thrushcross Grange—'

'It's being made ready for the New Year,' she broke in. 'This is Wuthering Heights, Miss Stewart.'

'If you will be good enough to inform Mr Heathcliff that Aspen Stewart is here to see him?'

'Mr Heathcliff isn't here,' she started to say.

'Mrs – what name do you bear?' I said impatiently.

'Ellen Dean, miss. Mrs Dean though I've never been wed. I was the housekeeper both here and later at Thrushcross Grange and now here again for a spell until the New Year.'

'Mr Heathcliff just beckoned to me from the upper window,' I said, 'so be so good as to admit me at once, Mrs Dean.'

The effect on her was both startling and frightening. Her plump face blanched and her mild eyes filled with something like horror as if she beheld something unspeakable.

'You'd best come in, miss,' was all she said.

I followed her into an immense chamber, open to the rafters, with a floor of scrubbed white stone and against the back wall a huge dresser, laden with pewter and silver, rising up to the bare beams from which joints of raw and cured meat, strings of onions and apples hung.

At one end of the housebody (for so I later learned it is named in these parts) a large fireplace was filled with a mixture of coal, peat and apple logs that blazed and leapt and sent out a sweet perfume.

There was a long table with chairs set about it and other chairs standing about and, half blocking what was obviously access to the inner recesses of the house, a high-backed settle carved with fruit and leaves. Under the arch of the dresser a large bitch suckled her litter and ignored me.

There were several bright rugs laid across the stone and on each side of the fireplace bookshelves were crammed with books.

'You'd best sit down, Miss Stewart,' she said. 'I was just making a pot of tea. Will you take a cup?'

I nodded and seated myself near the staircase that obviously climbed to the upper floors. In a moment, when my father chose to descend, he would see me sitting meekly there, in my grey gown and cloak with the little apples sparkling in my ears, and know that I had been obedient.

Mrs Dean went through to the back regions from whence came the clattering of dishes. Meanwhile I amused myself by looking about me, arriving at the opinion that though all was bright and well appointed, a man as wealthy as my father might have furnished more luxuriously. Then I remembered his other property in the valley and told myself that he would be taking his bride there, whoever she might be.

'Here we are, Miss Stewart! Tea and hot griddle cakes! If you are new to these parts you'll be feeling the cold!'

Mrs Dean bustled in with a large tray on which teacups and a pot of tea jostled with a plate of cakes so badly did her hands shake.

I went at once to assist her, taking the tray and setting it down on the table while I indicated she should sit down. She did so, taking a napkin from her apron and blotting her forehead with it, all the while sending nervous glances towards me.

'I am sorry to trouble you when you are not well,' I said.

'Oh, it's nothing, Miss Stewart!' she hastened to inform me. 'At my time of life one gets these sudden turns, dizziness and the like. Thank you. You're very kind.'

She gulped the tea I had poured as if it were water and she was dying of thirst in the Sahara. I was about to frame a question when an old man in breeches and black coat appeared beneath the inner archway, gurning towards us as he banged his stick on the ground.

'Ech, but heer's anither flaysome nowt t'infect thold place!' he said raspingly. 'Wimmen bring nowt but misery and moithering intae t'world!'

'Be off to your meeting!' Mrs Dean retorted, reviving somewhat, 'and don't go making a spectacle of yourself before the visitor!'

He glanced at us both and shambled off, shutting the front door with a crash.

'Take no notice of Joseph,' Mrs Dean advised. 'He's been servant here since he was a lad and he'll die in the ruins of this house yet!'

'Mr Heathcliff . . .' I began, casting a glance towards the staircase.

'You say your grandfather had business dealings with him?' She took a final gulp of tea and put the cup down again.

'In Ireland, yes. He went there when he was a very young man and my grandfather employed him.'

'So that was where he went!' she said softly. 'He never would say.'

'He has visited a few times over the years and two years ago, my grandfather having died, he invited me to visit should I ever be in this part of the world.'

'Miss Stewart, I'm afraid you've come on a fool's errand,' she said. 'Mr Heathcliff died back in April.'

I stood outside myself, watching as I slowly put down my cup on the table and said, very calmly as if the information imparted was only of trivial interest, 'Died? But he was not old, was he?'

'Short of forty I'd say,' she said. 'It's an odd coincidence but just a few days ago a gentleman who rented Thrushcross Grange a year ago, but left for the south before his tenancy was up, returned to pay what was owing and was equally surprised to learn of his demise. Of course he'd already heard much of Mr Heathcliff's previous history from me since he was interested and I was housekeeper there at that time. I'm surprised you never heard of the death yourself if Mr Heathcliff was in the habit of doing any business in Ireland.'

'Only rarely,' I said. 'In recent years his interests were separated from those of my late grandfather. 'You say the previous tenant—'

'Mr Lockwood,' she nodded.

'Mr Lockwood!'

The strange feeling of unreality faded as I stared at her.

'You don't know Mr Lockwood, do you?' she said in surprise.

'I believe we met briefly.'

'Now he could have told you a great deal about Mr Heathcliff because when he was at the Grange he got a severe chill and as he was recuperating, I whiled away several hours in telling him that master's story.'

'You know it all then. He never spoke of it to me or my grandfather.'

'If he knew all of it himself he never uttered,' she said. 'For my own part I know bits and pieces. Servants get to hear more than most and I was fortunate for my parents were employed by the Earnshaws; this house has been in the Earnshaw family for three centuries.'

'I saw the name and the date carved over the door.'

'Oh, the Earnshaws are a very old family,' she agreed. 'Now I was born in the same month as Mr Hindley Earnshaw, he being the son of old Mr Earnshaw and Mrs Earnshaw. Mrs Earnshaw put Hindley out to nurse with my mother for she

127

wasn't well after the birthing, so Hindley and I were foster brother and sister on that account. As I grew up I was always playing about the farm, sharing the children's lessons, Miss Catherine having been born about eight years later. When my own father died my mother moved to Halifax and I went to live with the Earnshaws as general maidservant.'

'You missed your mother?' I couldn't help asking.

'I went over now and then to see her. She lived to be eighty, so Halifax must've suited her.'

'Mr Heathcliff did mention that he'd been adopted,' I said.

'Aye he was and what possessed the master to take him in I'll never fathom! But off to Liverpool went Mr Earnshaw to transact some cattle buying and came back with a gypsy cub as sallow and sullen as you may imagine. And I can tell you that Mrs Earnshaw was furious to have a strange brat foisted upon her. She was for flinging it out of doors at once but the master could be very obstinate when he liked.'

'Liverpool is a good way off.'

'A hundred and twenty miles round trip.' She nodded.

'A long ride for a little boy.'

'Oh, the master walked the whole distance,' Mrs Dean said. 'He did it in three days and completed his business there. And he carried that child all the way here!'

I went on staring at her.

'He'd made enquiries,' she went on, 'but nobody would own to being parents or guardians of the boy.'

'That and his other business must've taken at least a day,' I mused. 'So he walked sixty miles a day then? Why not take one of the horses?'

'I've no idea.' A momentary puzzlement creased her brow. 'Nobody asked as far as I remember. I do recall the mistress wanted to fling the newcomer out of doors at once and the children were angry for he'd promised to buy Hindley a fiddle and

128

Catherine a whip and even me some apples and pears, but he lost the whip and the fiddle got broken and I never saw the apples and pears.'

'So he went shopping too,' I said. 'He must have had a very busy three days.'

'I didn't like the little ragamuffin myself,' she confessed. 'Mr Earnshaw told me to settle it with Hindley and Catherine but I put it on the stairs, hoping it'd be gone by morning. Instead of that it crept to the master's door and he was so angry at my unkindness that I was sent out of the house for a few days. These days I hope I'd be kinder but I was only fourteen then.'

'The master's room?'

'Mr and Mrs Earnshaw slept separate after Catherine's birth. He often had business to attend after dark and the mistress disliked being disturbed by his returning in the small hours. It was a bad beginning and it got worse.'

'How?'

If she thought my interest excessive she gave no sign. I marked her as a woman rather like Brigit who, having no real life of her own, existed on the fringes of other lives.

'Hindley hated the boy,' she said, 'but Catherine became his bosom companion, and very naughty the pair of them were. After Mr and Mrs Earnshaw died, Hindley who'd gone off to College came here with a wife and she bore a son and died within the year.'

'Another Hindley?' I prompted.

'Hareton, Miss Stewart. Not another Hindley in any respect for he'd taken to drink and Heathcliff was made to sleep in the stables and no decent family would visit us except the Lintons.'

'The name,' I said cautiously, 'sounds familiar.'

'Mr Edgar Linton and Catherine got wedded,' Ellen Dean told me. 'By then Heathcliff had upped sticks and run off – couldn't abide seeing our Miss Catherine being courted by anyone else. Took one of the horses and rode off and for three years we heard nowt of him. And you say he was in Ireland? Well, nobody troubled to go advertising for him but Miss Catherine took it hard. By the time he came back she was Mrs Linton of Thrushcross Grange. Excuse me! I think I hear Zillah. She was housekeeper here for a time and she often stops for a natter.'

'Is there somewhere I might wash my hands before I go?' I asked.

'There's a small room at the top of the stairs with a basin of water and a towel. I'll—'

'You greet your friend,' I said. 'The top of the stairs? I shall quickly find it.'

I left her to bustle into the back regions and went up the staircase past a closet, up a shorter flight of stairs and so reached the room that overlooked the courtyard. I must confess that I hesitated before lifting the latch and venturing in.

It was a large room, partly occupied by a huge cupboard that took up a third of the dusty space. It was not, however, a cupboard as I found on second glance but an interior space containing a wide bed with the house wall directly opposite me, its casements closed though only a remnant of tattered curtain hung from the rail. The inner ledge of the window was wide enough to serve as a shelf and was thick with dust. A narrow space at both sides of the stripped bed gave passage to the window. The whole was so thick with dust that I inadvertently sneezed and hastily muffled it lest Mrs Dean should hear, but she was safely in the kitchen by now, I reckoned, and heard nothing.

The rest of the chamber had been recently and hastily swept with fragments of dirt caught between the floorboards and the fireplace riotous with pebbles and bits of paper and twigs.

Once it must have been a handsome room with fine moulding on the ceiling and tapestries cut to shield the walls, but now the ceilings were blackened and cracked and the hangings hung drunkenly against stained walls and dead ashes spilled on to the carpet just within the door.

I knew it had been Catherine's and Heathcliff's room even before I bent and picked up the portrait that leant against one corner, its back towards the room. It was the same size and had the same frame, much tarnished now, as the portrait of the fair-haired young man I had seen at Thrushcross Grange.

I turned it in my hands and the face of a young girl stared out at me. A haughty face with a slight smile curving the full passionate mouth and mocking the spectator. The nose was high bridged and the long black hair only loosely confined by a narrow ribbon.

The eyes, I thought, were cat's eyes, slanting slightly above high cheekbones, dark eyes with flashes of amber about the iris, and thin black brows arched above the lids. The eyes stared at me, not with the indifference of painted orbs, but with a challenging expression lit by a hint of laughter. The eyes drew in the onlooker, held the intruder spellbound. There was drapery of some kind about the long white throat and a red flower, indifferently painted, in one corner.

This then, I thought, had been Heathcliff's Cathy. The one for whom he had sobbed in his sleep in a Dublin tavern was held now between my hands. I had a sudden urge to dash it against the wall or fling it into the grate but one thought restrained me. Had she not rejected him then I might never have been born. Not that I owed her any thanks for that!

From the enclosed bed behind me I heard a smothered giggle and, the edges of the portrait frame digging into my palms, swung round.

The stripped bed was occupied. Two children sat there, arms entwined, heads leaning together, their garments torn and stained. The girl had cat's eyes, dark and feline with an amber gleam and she showed pointed little white teeth in a goblin grin while the boy was sallow and wolf-eyed, his gaze devouring. I stood motionless, the breath catching in my throat as they each lifted the other's wrist to their mouth and bit into the flesh and sucked the droplets of blood that gathered along the broken skin, he from her and she from him. And even in my fear I saw how tenderly they sucked like babes fearful of hurting their mother and how, while the girl gazed at where I stood, for I cannot say she saw me, his eyes lingered on her with such intensity that he would have noticed nothing had I joined them on the bed.

I backed towards the door and, not shifting my gaze, set down the portrait, closed the door and went shiveringly down the stairs. I think I dipped my hands into the basin of cold water in the lower closet and dried them on the towel there but I'm not sure.

Mrs Dean came through from the kitchen quarters as I lifted the latch of the front door.

'I thought I heard you come down,' she said. 'Are you all right, Miss Stewart? You look very pale!'

'I think I walked a little too far today,' I said.

'Easily done! Mind you, they say walking's healthy! Now, shall I tell Mr Hareton and Miss Cathy that you called and will be returning?'

'I would like to hear the rest of Mr Heathcliff's history first,' I said, 'before I decide whether or not to continue business with whoever deals with matters now. Would tomorrow be too soon?'

'Miss Cathy and Mr Hareton are going over to Halifax to buy some new hangings for the Grange,' she told me. 'I'll not mention your call then?'

'Not yet. Mrs Dean, you looked uneasy when I arrived. I wondered why?'

'It's this house,' she said, flushing slightly. 'I was brought up here but since Mr Heathcliff . . . my eyes aren't what they were and that's a fact! But for an instant you reminded me of Mr Heathcliff himself and it gave me a bit of a turn.'

'A trick of the light,' I said. 'Thank you, Mrs Dean.'

I turned and crossed the courtyard and glanced up at the window as I barred the gate behind me. They were still there, older than their goblin childhoods, he holding her close to his side a little in the shadow but this time there was no beckoning hand. He was half turned towards her, hand stroking her cheek with infinite tenderness and as I hurried away only one question sobbed in my brain.

Why, oh why, had he not loved me like that?

ELEVEN

I walked back into the village across the moors, resisting the urge to turn my head to see if anyone was following me. Why would he trouble to come after me when he held his heaven in the crook of his arm? But the unfinished tale nagged at me as if I had found a map with the printing on it too faded to decipher.

When I reached the point where sundry streams joined to gush into the pool below the rocks, I trod carefully over the wet stepping-stones and reached the topmost pinnacle where I had seen the girl writing. She had been there just as she had stood on the steps of the house in the lane and called for Keeper, just as she had rushed past me on one of my first forays into the countryside, just as she had sat with a younger girl and written steadily near the blackcurrant bushes. But why she wrote and what she wrote I had no idea, nor whether she played any part in my father's story.

Seated there I looked about me, at the landscape lit by the gleams of an October afternoon sunshine, at the few scattered dwellings. I could see neither the house called Wuthering Heights nor the one called Thrushcross Grange from here, though the day was innocent of mist and the odd thought entered my head that these buildings only existed when I needed to see them and retreated from ordinary view.

If I didn't take care I would begin to imagine that I had been gifted with the sight. Brigit had talked about it sometimes, maintaining that her grandmother had possessed it and that it was both a blessing and a curse.

'For when my grandfather, God rest his soul, was thrown from his horse and killed outright, didn't she see the whole thing as it happened though he was ten miles off at the time and didn't that give her two extra hours of grief to add to her mourning?'

I stepped down from the high seat and followed the track into the lane that ran past the parson's house. This time I walked past rapidly without looking through the bars of the gate.

When I went into the inn I went up to change my shoes and then came down into the snug and ordered a meal. The walk had sharpened my appetite and my cheeks, glimpsed briefly in a mirror over the sideboard, were rosy. I did not look, I thought wryly, like a young woman who has just been told that her father has died. But then, when was Mr Heathcliff ever father to me? When did he dandle me on his knee and speak sorrowfully of the loss of my mother? When did he comb my long hair and sing jingling rhymes to make me laugh?

My feelings were not of sadness but of a cold, bitter anger. At the last when he might have acknowledged me as his daughter then he had slipped away. Even as I thought that a shadow fell across me and I half turned to ask the maid who had just brought in a dish of potatoes to bring a tumbler of water, but the shadow was gone with nothing to account for its presence and there was no sign of the maid.

Was that how it was to be then? Half-seen phantoms, questions that remained unanswered, shadows where no solid object stood? I rang the little bell on my table and sharply ordered the maidservant when she finally appeared, to hurry with the meat before the vegetables were stone-cold.

Mr Heathcliff had died according to Mrs Dean, but I knew now that death itself could be a deception. Those who had died, those who had never yet existed thronged the corners of every room, sat writing in small gardens or on the moors, inhabited houses where the inhabitants fondly imagined they dwelt alone. And they strewed clues for the bafflement of others: the half-forgotten conversations of a nursemaid, a ring of bird bones, a pair of ruby apples, a tearstained note hidden in a drawer and discovered too late, a journal with a four-leafed shamrock pressed in its pages.

Later, having just finished a glass of wine and a dish of toast, I came through into the taproom to find a middle-aged man, cap in hand, waiting to speak to me.

'Miss Stewart? Hatton Binns, miss, at your service. You want to hire a horse I'm told?'

'I understand that you have horses you hire out?'

'Yes, miss, but the three of them are hired out over Shibden way,' he said apologetically. 'Not wanting to disoblige a visitor I asked around and in the course of making enquiry met Mr Earnshaw – Mr Hareton Earnshaw that is – and he said he was sure Mrs Heathcliff would hire out one of her own. She's never averse to mekking a bit of brass, so he spoke to her and came over with a nifty little mare and I brought her here if you can pay for a week in advance. I'll see Mrs Heathcliff gets the money and I'm to give you a receipt.'

'I will see the mare first,' I said.

'She's tethered out front,' Mr Binns told me and held open the door with the kind of rough courtesy I had seen in these parts before.

She was a pretty mare, well groomed and, judging by the welcoming muzzle she offered, not mean-spirited.

The bargain concluded, I invited Mr Binns to take a tumbler of ale before he departed, an invitation he accepted with alacrity.

'Not that I'm in the habit of taking strong liquor as a rule, mind,' he said, settling down the tumbler after quaffing half its contents. 'Zillah – that's my sister – and I are joined Methodists and strong drink is frowned upon something fierce, but Zillah is more joined than mesen if tha gets the drift and a drop of ale is always welcome. Your good health!'

He raised the tumbler again but suddenly set it down, his eyes sliding past me with an expression in them difficult to define.

'Is anything wrong?' I asked.

'Nowt int'world!' he said hastily. 'It were only . . . have you stayed in these parts before?'

'This is my first visit to England.'

'Just for a minute I thought we'd met before,' he said.

'Oh?'

He was staring at me, his ale apparently forgotten.

'You reminded me of someone,' he said, and frowned again.

'Oh? Whom?'

I fully expected him to say Mr Heathcliff but he said, 'I hope as tha'll not tek offence, miss, but your eyes are . . . there was a gypsy woman used to tell fortunes hereabouts, Mag her name was or so she said, used to come during harvest time and camp up near Penistone Crags. Good-looking in her time. Had very dark sparkling eyes. I had my fortune told once with some of the lads, all rubbish, miss, for none of it came true, but it were a bit of a lark! Pardon me for mentioning it!'

'Does she still come?' I queried.

'I've not seen her in a year or more. She'll be getting on in years now anyways, close on sixty. Thank you kindly for the ale, miss. Now I'll just sign this receipt and get back to Zillah. Mrs Heathcliff will have the money first thing.'

'And the mare is called. . . ?'

'Beg pardon, miss! Her name's Minty; her dam was named Minna and her sire was Tyrone, one of Mr Heathcliff's horses.

You may have heard that he died.'

'Yes, indeed I did. Thank you, Mr Binns.'

I shook hands with him warmly and saw him out, deciding that if any closer connection between Mr Heathcliff and myself were to be revealed it would be at my behest and not at anyone else's. Then I asked the landlady to put Minty in the stables at the back of the inn and took myself upstairs again.

Pictures were cohering in my mind but not for long. No sooner did one become clear than it dissolved into another, edges blurring, nothing to point the way clearly ahead. I fell asleep with Catherines and Lintons and Earshaws buzzing in my brain like a swarm of bees whose queen has deserted them.

In the morning I ate a leisurely breakfast, went into the stables and had Minty saddled up. It was good to feel her beneath me as I cleared the stile and trotted out on to the open moor. It was a fine day too, the ground dipping and rising in swells of brown and auburn, the sky a pale azure and the sun warming the landscape into vibrant life.

I was further heartened when I reached Wuthering Heights to find Mrs Dean hanging some linen on the line.

'Miss Stewart! It's good to see you again,' she said cordially, coming to unbar the gate. 'Let me just take Minty into the stables. Miss Catherine – Mrs Heathcliff prefers old Minna but Minty has been her pony since her childhood. Come and have some tea, Miss Stewart, for Joseph has gone over to Sowdens to buy some feed and he makes a day's journey out of every errand.'

'Is he a relation of the family?' I enquired, following her when she had tethered the pony into a warm, bright kitchen.

'Lord bless you but no!' she exclaimed, laughing. 'It's my belief he was created along with the house for surely no mother ever owned to him! Nay, Joseph's been here as lad and man and will die in this place. He's a sanctimonious old hypocrite but let's not sour the morning in talk of him. Are you well lodged at the inn still?'

'Very comfortably,' I said.

'And you're relishing your taste of Yorkshire?'

She busied herself with the teapot and a dish of scones, bearing them finally on a large tray into the front chamber with its lofty roof and massive dresser. Within the arch of the latter a huge dog growled softly.

'Hush, Juno! the young lady'll not harm your pups,' Mrs Dean scolded. 'Now, Miss Stewart, you just help yourself. A ride over the moors always sharpens the appetite.'

'Indeed it does,' I agreed. 'But I hope my calling again doesn't interfere with your own routine?'

'To tell you the truth, Miss Stewart,' she confessed, 'I am glad of the company. I don't much like being here alone now, even in daylight, not since Mr Heathcliff's death.'

'Oh?'

I looked at her but she made a great business of pouring the tea.

'So Catherine Earnshaw wed Mr Edgar Linton?' I prompted at last.

'And were very happy together,' she said somewhat defensively, 'but then Heathcliff turned up, looking quite the gentleman, and he wed Miss Isabella Linton though on his side there was no love and her infatuation died a rapid death. She left him before their child was born and spent the rest of her life in London.'

I thought of the letter I had found and the pale, fair-haired girl who had glided to the portrait of her brother in the deserted Grange.

'She had a son,' Mrs Dean was continuing, 'but his father never laid eyes on the poor weakling until after Miss Isabella died. My Miss Catherine, Mrs Linton I should say, bore a daughter and died of it less than six months after Mr Heathcliff returned – and you say he was in Ireland? He never told how he came by his money or his fine clothes.'

'Business dealings,' I said, feeling suddenly uneasy without quite knowing why.

'So it's a cuckoo's tale,' she said with a faint sigh as if she had suspected as much. 'Mr Heathcliff died owning Wuthering Heights and Thrushcross Grange, and yet he didn't bargain for Hareton falling in love with his son's widow, for he forced my Miss Cathy to wed that sickly creature only weeks before he died. Yes, Mr Heathcliff cast off his beginnings and became a man of property though in the end he died too.'

'How' I asked.

'Just faded,' she said briefly, the uneasiness coming into her face again.

'And I must complete my ride on Minty,' I said, taking the hint. 'Thank you for the tea and the scones, Mrs Dean. I'm sorry to leave you alone here but—'

'Oh, I shall go out and sit in the open for a while,' she said with what seemed rather like forced cheerfulness. 'Happen Joseph might not be too long.'

I glanced up towards that certain window as we left the house but it was shuttered and I noticed that Mrs Dean never followed the direction of my glance with her own eyes. Yet as she opened the gate she said abruptly, 'Mr Heathcliff was a villain, Miss Stewart, but when he were a lad something about him touched the heart. I never could explain it.'

'You've made me so welcome,' I said, 'that perhaps I could prevail on you to have lunch with me at the inn tomorrow. Your account of Mr Heathcliff and his beginnings is most interesting.'

'I did think as how you were uncommonly struck,' she said.

'I've recently come into my grandfather's legacy,' I said

blandly, 'so naturally I'm interested in all his business associates. Good day to you.'

I waved my hand cheerfully as I rode away on Minty. It was still fine with a warmth in the breeze that gave the lie to Yorkshire always being a cold place. I let Minty have her head and was scarcely surprised when, instead of making for Gimmerton, she swerved aside towards the lower valley where Thrushcross Grange stood.

I wasn't averse to seeing the house again now that I knew a little more about its previous owners and so slackened the reins and let her take me along her preferred path, descending the gradual slopes past a peaty marsh until I saw the walls and the trees and the chimneys behind them of the Grange.

This time I rode boldly in with an excuse on my lips and was on the curve of the path before it widened into a drive when an old man in shirtsleeves and breeches with a basket of apples in his hand came round the corner and stopped dead on seeing me.

'I'm afraid there's nobody at home,' he said.

'My pony chose the way,' I said.

'Of course! It's Minty! She was foaled here three years back,' he said, advancing to stroke her nose, a gesture she received with every sign of pleasure. 'I'm Robert, Miss. . . ?'

'Aspen Stewart,' I told him. 'I'm in the neighborhood on some business connected with my late grandfather's estate. There are some fine old buildings hereabouts.'

'And Thrushcross Grange is one of the finest, miss,' he said promptly. 'I've worked here as boy and man and the Lintons who owned the property, you couldn't find a more genteel family.'

'I've had the pleasure of meeting Mrs Dean,' I said, dismounting and handing him the reins. 'I believe she was housekeeper here once?'

'Aye she was, when the late Mrs Linton was first wed,' he affirmed. 'She died when her girl was born and Ellen Dean stayed on as nurse and houseekeeper for nigh on sixteen years. Sometimes fancied herself as the mistress if you ask me!'

'You didn't like her? She seemed pleasant enough to me,' I said.

'Inclined to take advantage.' He shook his grey head. 'Mind you she was always a sensible body. She started off up at the Heights; that was the Earnshaw place further up the valley.'

'A great gaunt building with thorn trees slanting against the wind? Yes, I have seen it.'

'A rough place for rough people,' he said with another doleful shake of his head. 'Ellen Dean would always have it that the Earnshaws were equal to the Lintons but it was never so. Old Earnshaw was a farmer – oh, he knew a thing or two about horses and about women too if you ask me!'

'I was wondering,' I broke in, 'if you could spare some water for the horse. To be honest I'd not be averse to a mug of water myself.'

'I should've thought of it myself,' he said instantly. 'I'll put Minty in her old stable with some water and a bit of feed. The house is closed up mainly and won't be lived in proper until the New Year when Miss Catherine who wed Mr Heathcliff's son and is his widow now marries her cousin, Mr Hareton. It was rented out for a spell but Mr Hareton and Miss Cath— Mrs Heathcliff I ought to say, want to make this their permanent home. Come along in, do!'

He was obviously now the caretaker here and equally obviously bored with his own company. Soon, with Minty settled in one of the stables, he led the way via the door I'd previously entered into a large pleasant kitchen.

'I've just brewed some tea,' he said. 'Nothing like tea for refreshing the spirits! Yes, over fifty years I've served the Lintons.

Very warm people in the sense of holding property; old Mr
Linton had an East India inheritance and they were very particular as to manners and gentility. You might've noticed my
own accent isn't as loud as some round here.'

'Neither has Mrs Dean a strong accent,' I couldn't avoid
pointing out.

'True,' he conceded. 'Oh, the Earnshaws could speak well
enough but teach a parrot to talk and it don't turn human. Old
Hareton Earnshaw – I mean the grandfather of the present Mr
Hareton – now he could speak soft when he'd anything to gain
and he wasn't bad-hearted. He took in Ellen Dean whose
mother nursed Mr Hindley along with her own child. Mind you,
I've always had a bit of a wonder about Ellen Dean. No sign of
a father and her mother went off to Halifax and Ellen was
reared at the Heights but there, that's just idle gossip! And then
Mr Earnshaw ups and walks to Liverpool – Liverpool I'm
asking you – and brings back the gypsy boy.'

'Heathcliff,' I said, accepting the cup of tea.

'Aye, spoilt and petted him above his own son. Bred bad feeling in the family.'

'And his origins unknown,' I said.

'Aye, but I've my own opinion on that score!'

He winked the sly, knowing wink of the very old.

'And Miss Earnshaw married Mr Edgar Linton?' I prompted.

'Aye. She were eighteen and Mr Edgar just twenty-one and
both sets of parents dead, Hindley a widower with the baby,
Hareton, and nobody knowing where Heathcliff had run off.'

'And after three years he returned to marry—'

'Miss Isabella Linton. Miss Isabella of all people, who
might've had any young buck in the county.'

'Mrs Dean said—'

'Ah now!' He shook his head. 'Ellen Dean's always been a bit
of a gossip. Now I don't go nattering to strangers – you being

interested is different of course – but yes, Miss Isabella was stuck all of a heap by his handsome looks as you might say. Yet the first time she laid eyes on him when he was a young lad she said he looked like the fortune-telling gypsy who'd stolen her tame pheasant! Now that same gypsy slattern tried to make me have my fortune read once, me who reads the lessons in church!'

'You don't approve of gypsies?' I said.

'Well, there's a place for everything on this earth,' he said, 'but I never fathomed why God invented gyppos! Mind, when she were young she were a bit of a good-looker: black hair and a mouth like – no, it's my belief gyppos were made out of odds and ends of leftovers the good Lord wasn't sure what to do about! Anyway she went off years ago. Murdered probably. Most gyppos get murdered. It's a known fact!'

I said nothing since there seemed no adequate answer to his rather novel point of view. For a few moments we sipped the rest of our cooling tea in silence while the empty house brooded about us.

'Miss Linton running off must've upset the household very much,' I said at last, hoping far some further revelation.

'That it did! And Nelly taking it upon herself not to tell Mr Edgar that his wife were in a frenzy or that Miss Isabella had run off with that devil, Heathcliff. She let him in to see her body too, the night before the funeral. Thought I didn't notice she'd left the long window unlatched! Mr Edgar had gone to bed – exhausted with watching – and I kept a sharp look out from under the stairs and in comes Mr Heathcliff, shirtsleeves and his black hair hanging loose, and lifts the veil from Mrs Linton's face and it were a funny thing, Miss Stewart, but when I peeked in, and he'd not have heard an army marching through, he were just kneeling by the coffin, stroking her face like you might stroke the feathers of a little bird, and he kept saying over and over, "Do hold me for a moment, Cathy. Do hold me just once more." And her cold and stiff for three days! And he took out a little knife and cut off a lock of his hair and put it into the locket she had about her neck, and then he got up and went away somewheres. I'm glad he did for I'd not have had the heart to throw him out.'

I said nothing. I sat mutely in that big kitchen in the house where my father had intruded and renewed his relationship with Cathy, as he had always called her, and been ejected and stolen away Isabella whose wistful ghost still wandered, hoping for forgiveness from the brother she had disobeyed, and met for the last time with his other self and returned to gaze on her dead face and see mirrored there his own features, and I wondered if he had ever told my mother the tale, grinding each word home like a hammer blow because he hated the whole world save for his lost self, and I still said nothing. I could only sit mutely while old Robert took the tea-cups away and pottered about the untenanted space, oblivious to what still glided there just out of sight.

And I wished that I was in the glen at Imdel and that I could give my father a different answer than the silence with which I had greeted his last request to me, that someone hold him for just a moment. And I knew my answer would always have been silence.

TWELVE

The next day the fine weather continued though there was an added crispness in the air. I had taken my leave of Robert, slipping a discreet tip into his hand, and left him to caretake in the mansion he believed was empty save when the cleaning women came. For the remainder of the day I had rested, dropping now and then into a fitful doze through which it seemed to me that someone was calling from a great distance but could not make themselves heard or unrderstocd.

The new day brought Ellen Dean according to her promise, looking sadly tired and flustered.

'Truth is,' she confided, 'the walk's wearied me more than I thought it would. I've put on a mite too much weight though my housekeeping duties are heavy enough.'

'I've ordered pigeon pie with vegetables which we shall enjoy in the snug,' I told her. 'Then you shall ride Minty back to the Heights. I shall lead her.'

'That's very good of you, Miss Stewart,' she beamed, 'for the truth is that I was never much of a rider. Walking used to be my pleasure, walking and reading. It'll be a real treat also to sit down to a meal I haven't cooked myself!'

The pigeon pie with its gilded leaves of pastry and the potatoes and greens having been served and my guest having agreed to imbibe half a glass of ale we settled down, the snug being empty save for ourselves.

Midway through our repast she put down her knife and fork and sent me a long steady look. 'You're mightily interested in Mr Heathcliff's story,' she said.

'He had business dealings with my late grandfather, Ronald Stewart,' I said. 'I believe their parts were separated by mutual consent before my grandfather died but one likes to check on all angles. I met Mr Heathcliff once or twice when he visited Ireland and found his manner not in the common run.'

'With his history who could expect otherwise?' she said. 'I'd a pitying fondness for him when he was a lad but that passed for he grew up cruel and mean.'

'And now he is dead,' I said as casually as I could.

'A whole generation gone,' she nodded. 'Miss Catherine and Mr Edgar and Mr Hindley and poor young Linton, Mr Heathcliff's son by Miss Isabella—'

'A tangle of marriages and deaths,' I ventured.

'Aye, cousin marrying cousin,' she nodded.

'And now Mr Heathcliff is gone too. How did he die? He seemed healthy enough when he visited my grandfather in Ireland.'

'Flourished like the green bay tree as the saying goes,' she nodded, 'save for his nerves, which were always nearer the surface of his skin than others though he'd not admit it. Cool above and torn to tatters below.'

'He fell ill?' I pursued.

She shook her head slightly.

'Became quieter and lost some weight,' she said after a moment. 'My Miss Cathy and Hareton were beginning to be friends but Mr Heathcliff didn't seem to notice properly what was going on around him the last few weeks. It was near the end of March when he became—'

'Sick?' I suggested as she paused.

'More excited really,' she said slowly. 'Seemed in a kind of a dream most of the time – no, that's not it! Seemed as if he was waiting for someone or something. And when we moved into April I did notice his breathing was changing, becoming slower with long pauses between as if he had to keep reminding himself to breathe. And one thing I know for sure, for four days before his death he neither ate nor drank a thing!'

'You didn't call a doctor?'

'It wasn't ny place.' She flushed slightly. 'He said he was perfectly well but he spent most of his time up in the old bedroom – you'll not have seen it of course – but he and the first Cathy slept there together when they were children. He asked me to sit with him there one night for company but his manner was so strange that I made some excuse. He went up there alone and in the morning he was dead.'

I said nothing. I sipped my ale and all I could frame in my mind were the words: he wanted company.

'Would you like something else?' I asked at last, indicating her plate.

'Not a thing, Miss Stewart!' she exclaimed. 'That was a fine meal and I'm obliged to you. But time's getting on and I've the walk back—'

'You shall ride Minty,' I told her, 'and I will lead her and ride her back.'

After a little more half-hearted protesting she agreed and I went up to don my boots and cloak and came down to find her already seated on the pony, her skirts tucked up.

'Do you know the Reverend Charnock?' I asked as we went down the lane.

'Only by sight really,' she admitted. 'I'm not a regular church-goer myself though my late master, Mr Edgar Linton, always went on Sundays and held regular prayers for family and staff over at the Grange. The Earnshaws never troubled much about worship, though when they did go it was usually to the old church near the peat bog but that's almost ruined now. Why do you ask about Mr Charnock?'

'He seemed quite pleasant,' I said as casually as I could.

I did not mention the girl who had called the name of Keeper into the night.

'Where is Mr Heathcliff buried?' I asked instead.

'According to his own wishes, without benefit of clergy, on the edge of the heath near the old church,' she told me. 'Mr Edgar and Miss Catherine lie there also. It's a lonely place.' She gave a slight shiver as she spoke and I judged it wiser to speak of other things until we were within sight of the Heights when she slid awkwardly from Minty's back, saying, 'It's only a step from here, Miss Stewart. Were Mr Heathcliff and your grandfather close?'

'Business associates,' I repeated.

'I'd best be going or Joseph will be carrying on at me for wasting time gadding on the moor,' she said.

'Ignore him,' I counselled.

'Easier said than done,' she retorted. 'Thank you again, Miss Stewart. The Heights is no more than a mile from here and that's no distance even for me! Will you be paying another visit there while you're in the neighbourhood, Miss Stewart? I ask because if there's any legal matter to be settled then Mr Green was Mr Heathcliff's lawyer so he'd likely be able to set you straight on most matters. You won't repeat. . . ?'

'Not a word,' I said. 'I merely desired to know the background to Mr Heathcliff's life before I gave my own lawyer instructions. I will call again in a day or two if I might?'

'You can meet my Miss Cathy then,' she said, a smile lifting the sadness from her face. 'The bonniest lass that ever was! She went over to the Grange today to match the curtains up.'

'With Mr Hareton?'

'Well, no, miss.' She grimaced slightly. 'Mr Hareton isn't much interested in the hanging of curtains and such like and Miss Cathy went off in a bit of a huff! Nothing serious and it'll be mended by nightfall but she's a quick temper and he cannot abide being ordered around. But the loving cancels all that out you know. Goodbye.'

She took her things from the saddlebag and waved her hand as she struck out across the slopes.

I stayed where I was for a spell, gazing about me at the dips and folds of the ground. The Heights wasn't visible from where I stood and the feeling that had swept over me before, of places only being there when they were needed, engulfed me again. If I stood here long enough, I too might melt into the landscape becoming one with the grass and the rock and the beck far below that tumbled towards the peaty marsh.

I remounted Minty and rode at an ambling pace with no clear destination in mind.

Ellen Dean might fondly imagine that Mr Heathcliff was safely interred. I had seen him beckoning to me, had seen him in his childhood intimacy with his cat-eyed Cathy and with his arm about her waist as he stood in the window of the upper room. How he had died remained a puzzle, though my mind returned to the comment he had made about the business in which he had engaged with my grandfather. That he had died before his plans were completed into action seemed very plain to me.

He would never have wanted the children of his old enemies, Edgar Linton and Hindley Earnshaw, to mate. Hindley Earnshaw had degraded him from adopted son to yokel and Edgar Linton had tempted away the girl he had loved and begotten a daughter on her.

He had spoken at our last meeting for a moment or two of

150

other plans, plans for the lad he had in turn reduced to farm-hand yet still retained an unwilling affection for. And he had invited me to visit him when I had attained my majority.

I had ridden close to the beck as it foamed and chortled over its bed of soil and stones. When I glanced behind me I could see the great rocks of Penistone Crags overhanging the valley, not black today but gilded by the October sun into a dozen different shades of gold.

And then I saw him. It was the second time I had beheld him. He and the girl with yellow ringlets had descended the steep path from the crags, passing me without seeing me, teasing and laughing as they came, each oblivious to everything save the other.

Now he was alone, shirt off, kneeling by the beck and splashing water over himself. I sat on Minty and looked at him, at the drops of water that gleamed like moonstones as they coursed down his back, at the broad brown shoulders and the movement of the muscles under the skin as he raised his arms and stretched into the sunshine.

His hair was as black as my own, cut carelessly to just above his shoulders, the strands dripping too and, as he pushed back one long lock he half turned his head and I saw the jutting nose and the square chin and the slight curve of his cheek.

He rose then, long-legged and, as Minty gave a little snicker, turned and looked up. Sunlight glinted on the thick chest hair that tapered into a v above the waistband of his breeches and sunlight gilded the tips of the long black lashes that outlined the dark eyes with their amber gleam.

Those eyes had mocked out of his Aunt Catherine's face, and they returned my own gaze steadily with a faint surprise in them as if he recognized my features from somewhere partly forgotten.

I nodded slightly as if to seal a bargain and wheeled Minty

about and rode her hard to where the crags towered up into the sky.

There was a woman on the lower slopes of Penistone. She was a tall woman and age had not bent her shoulders though her brown face was seamed. As I rode past her I saw the long grey plaits hanging at each side of her face and the little apples tied to the end of each plait that winked and sparkled in the October brightness.

THIRTEEN

There was a letter waiting for me when I returned to the inn. I paid the frank, mentally noting that it would be deducted from Mr Alistair's bill, and took it upstairs to read.

The neat copperplate reminded me of the trim, spare figure of the lawyer whom my grandfather had always and with good reason trusted and for the space of a heartbeat I wanted to be in my grandfather's study again, listening and learning as they went over the accounts together.

Dear Miss Stewart,

By now you will have heard of the death of Mr Heathcliff, which information reached me only a few days ago. As you are already aware your late grandfather and Mr Heathcliff had certain business interests in common which were later separated each into its component part. With Mr Heathcliff these several years I have had nothing to do, but I have dealt with your grandfather's side of the export business to the best of my ability through the good offices of the Dublin agent. It has been a three-way traffic as the goods are first imported to Dublin where they are refined before export to London. I need hardly add that such transactions are legal according to the letter of the law, and comprise a third of your total income. I would also add, as a friend, that I see no necessity for you to acquaint yourself with the precise details of the transactions.

The rents have been collected and I enclose a statement. I also enclose a list of repairs recently carried out on the roof of the main house and to the north barn. I took the liberty of paying the workmen in your absence.

All in the house are well though Brigit has had some trouble with a pain in her knee, but that has eased and she asks me to convey her love to you and to enquire when you intend returning.

I must also send you the good wishes of the Brunty family who wish to be remembered to you. Hugh Brunty seems a little better since the rains have dispersed and indeed I understand that his ailment is chronic rather than a source of immediate danger, for which we must be thankful. He informs me that his eldest son, Patrick, has entered upon his studies at Cambridge University and has some thoughts of altering his surname slightly in order to the better accord with English usage.

I await any further instructions you may have and send my own good wishes to you and hopes for your speedy and safe return to your native shores.

Yours respectfully and sincerely,
G. Alistair

I sat for a long while thinking and then I drafted a reply and went down to find the postman. I found him nattering to the woman whom I had noticed serving behind the counter in the apothecary's shop opposite the inn, and ordered that the letter be sent post-haste to Ireland by the next boat and conveyed at once to Mr Alistair. Then I took my habitual slow stroll along the lane but the garden beyond the barred gates was empty and its little lawn only roughly cut.

A week at least would pass if not longer before I might expect Mr Alistair's reply. Meanwhile a long evening stretched ahead of me, a time in which to reflect further on my plans. Of one thing I was sure. My father had been cheated by death from further-ing his own plans and I believed that I knew what those plans had been. And I determined that death would not cheat him of obtaining what had been among his last wishes. So I had a light repast brought to my room and sat afterwards for a spell, think-ing.

Of the causes of Mr Heathcliff's strange death I felt I had some inkling but whether I would ever breathe them to anyone else I had no notion. It seemed to me that certain things ought not to be looked at too nearly. A third of an income was a great sum to abandon.

The next day I went shopping in the village, buying a jar of honey here, a bolt of worsted there. I was served politely, charged honestly and, since my sojourn in Gimmerton was proving to be a longish one, some of the villagers even nodded to me and muttered a gruff good day as they went past. I thought one or two even glanced at me sharply, met my gaze, and for an instant seemed puzzled as if they felt they ought to know me, but that might have been my imagination.

On the Sabbath I attended a service at the church, not want-ing the Reverend Charnock to reach the conclusion that the visitor was an out-and-out heathen, and also hoping that some-one from the congregation might open up to me.

The interior of the building was dark and the high-backed pews afforded scant glimpses of the worshippers. Not that they themselves were of particular interest when one saw them: women in dark shawls and bonnets, men in funereal black or rough tweed with their hats and caps in their hands, a long row of children squashed up together under the eye of a strict-looking sexton. I wondered how many of them had known Mr Heathcliff in person or heard of the feuding between the Earnshaws and Lintons, and if anyone would be inclined to gossip with a stranger as Mrs Dean, in particular, had done with me.

The Reverend Charnock inclined his head slightly as he saw me seated solitary in one of the few empty pews below the pulpit. I bowed my own head to hide a smile, thinking how my father would have quickly disabused him of the notion that here was a brand plucked from the burning. He gave out a hymn and then read the lesson which seemed to me nicely read but in itself not of great interest.

I must have lost concentration for a moment because the next words I heard were uttered in a different voice, a clear voice with the unmistakable intonation of the Northern Irish albeit slightly muted.

There was evidently a guest speaker for the Reverend Charnock had stepped down from the pulpit and a tall, thin clergyman with greying red hair had taken his place. I stared at him, feeling a sudden flurry of bewilderment maze my brain for I could've sworn that the newcomer was Pat Brunty some twenty odd years on. I marked the handsome nose and the light blue eyes.

There were several children in the square box pew just below the pulpit. I saw them indistinctly for the sides of the pew were high, reminding me somewhat of the boxbed I had seen at Wuthering Heights, but I craned my neck slightly to behold heads of light and dark hair, one with neat pigtails, another with frizzy red hair about a little goblin face.

'For the Lord saith seventy times seven hast thou transgressed and been forgiven!' the preacher was saying. 'The Lord's forgiveness is vast indeed but it is not unending. Those of you who have entertained an impure thought or cheated a trades-man or slighted a neighbour take heed lest you have just committed the four hundredth and ninety-first sin against the Almighty! Do not lean for ever against hope of His mercy!'

The little red-haired lad in the pew below the pulpit all of a sudden popped up like a jack in the box and screwed his face into an extraordinary grimace at me. I puffed my cheeks and put out my tongue at him but before he could respond a bonneted woman who also sat in the pew leaned to shift him about and administer a small shake at the same time.

I hoped she hadn't noticed my own less than adult response and hastily bent my head to my prayerbook and became engrossed in its gilt-edged pages and when I ventured to raise my eyes again the Reverend Charnock was back in the pulpit and the pew below was vacant.

'Good morning, Miss Stewart, a pleasure to see you here,' he said formally when the service was done.

'As I am spending more time in the neighbourhood than I thought I would,' I said, 'I thought it incumbent on me to attend service. You have a large congregation.'

'Satisfactorily so,' he agreed. 'Of course many attend the Methodist services but we must remember we are all part of the One.'

'I wondered . . .' I hesitated and then plunged on. 'I wondered if you were acquainted with the late Mr Heathcliff?'

'Not with anyone of that name,' he said.

'He died in the spring.'

'Then he must've been a newcomer for I cannot bring him to mind. Good morning, Mrs Brown! And how are you faring?'

I stared at him as he turned to greet another parishioner just emerging from the church. Then I reminded myself that the Earnshaws had been remiss in Sunday observance and that my father had been buried without benefit of clergy.

I couldn't help reflecting, as I took a short, solitary walk along the lane to where the stile afforded access to the fields and the moors rising beyond, that these people, shut in by hill and bog and the vagaries of the weather, were a strange tribe, bred from whetstone and flint, yet each one an individual, some, not many, ready to talk to a stranger, others more distantly polite and others simply ignoring me as if I walk among them invisible, a ghost amid ghosts.

I longed then for Brigit's loving scolding and for the calm, kindly tones of Hugh Brunty whose son, Patrick, was now studying at Cambridge and definitely not in Gimmerton preaching about sin!

'I understand you were enquiring about Mr Heathcliff?'

The voice was a new one and I turned about on the stile to see an elderly gentleman walking towards me, hat in hand, a small dog frisking at his heels.

'Yes,' I said.

'I am Dr Kenneth, Miss Stewart,' he informed me.

He spoke as if I might be acquainted with the name but I stared at him blankly.

'You are a relation?' he pursued, still staring at me.

'Possibly,' I evaded.

'I was never aware he had any blood relations,' he said, looking puzzled.

'Possibly a distant connection,' I murmured.

'I was but newly qualified when I came to settle here,' he said, throwing a stone for the little dog to chase. 'The Earnshaws were second only to the Lintons in this district and both families gave me their patronage. I attended nearly all the families and was present at many deathbeds. A physician cannot save all.'

'You were present at Mr Heathcliff's dying?'

He shook his head.

'At old Mr Earnshaw's funeral – he died of a heart attack quite peaoefully – and when Mr Hindley Earnshaw's wife produced young Hareton I had the sad duty of warning him that he'd not keep her long. I was right for the poor thing fluttered and faded. Mr Hindley turned to the bottle for consolation and Miss Earnshaw – Miss Catherine that was – married Mr Edgar Linton but she died when the younger Miss Cathy was born. Very sad.'

'Your patients,' I said lightly, 'seem to have a habit of dying on you.'

'She'd been ill before with a kind of brain fever,' he said. 'That was after Mr Heathcliff came back. Mr Hindley died of the drink or so I was told for I wasn't called to attend to him. I thought he might've made old bones but drink's a fearsome enemy. Anyway Mr Heathcliff had all Mr Hindley's notes to hand – card -playing and gambling – so he took over the Heights. Little Miss Cathy grew up at Thrushcross Grange and then Miss Isabella Linton, who'd run off to wed Mr Heathcliff, ran off to London and we had twelve years peace until she died and her boy, Linton Heathcliff, was brought north and claimed by his father. Weakly, ma'am. All the Lintons had a tendency to consumption. He died weeks after he wed Miss Cathy and left Thrushcross Grange, which was entailed to him, to his father, so Mr Heathcliff ended up rich.'

'But how did he end up?' I said impatiently. 'How did he die?'

'I was never called in to attend him,' Dr Kenneth said. 'In fact I saw him only a few days before walking on the moors. He seemed healthy enough, excited almost with his eyes glinting and his hands trembling. I hailed him but he didn't seem to notice me. A few days later that old fool Joseph – he's servant up at the Heights – came hamering at my door to say the master was dead and there'd be feasting in hell that day. I sometimes think that Joseph is heading fast for the lunatic asylum never

mind feasting in hell! Anyway I went over to Wuthering Heights
and there was young Hareton weeping over a grinning corpse
and Nelly Dean white as a ghost. There was nothing I could do.'

'I see,' I said.

'And you think he might've been a relative of yours?' He
whistled to the dog and gave me a long, piercing look.

'It's a faint possibility,' I said mendaciously.

'Well, there's property involved,' he said. 'Mr Heathcliff left
no will so both Withering Heights and Thrushcross Grange
revert to the original heirs and as Miss Cathy and Mr Hareton
are to wed at the New Year all will be sweet as honey in the
dovecot.'

'Yes,' I said.

He gave me another keen stare and said abruptly, 'It would
be a pity if fresh trouble were to land on that young couple after
all the sadness of the past.'

'It would indeed,' I acknowledged and he raised his hat,
turned and went back along the lane, the little dog bounding at
his heels.

I climbed the stile and set off across the moor, conscious that
I had been warned off quite politely but definitely.

It was a clear day with a glitter in the air as if myriads of
small spirits cavorted there and the last of the browning heather
caught fire from the brightness and glowed russet with here and
there a pale wisp of green.

I strolled for half an hour, turning over in my mind various
possibilities. I thought that I could make a shrewd guess at why
my father had died. That commodity which he and my grandfather had imported at great profit was a bad master. I had
heard of the dens in London and in Dublin where men and
women lay stupified under its influence while others chattered
nonsense or sat, trembling from head to foot, while the noxious
fumes rose about them.

A figure was striding across the moor towards me. The breeze had caught her hood and blown it backward to reveal the dark, red glinted hair held back carelessly by Spanish combs and I saw plainly the high-bridged nose and the pouting lips.

'Keeper! Here, boy!'

I knew that piercingly sweet voice from before. She passed within yards of me but when I turned to look after her, only the russet of the dying heather stirred and bore no imprint of her passing.

FOURTEEN

It takes a good deal of planning to arrange an accidental meeting. For two or three days following my conversation with Dr Kenneth I rode Minty out on the moors, watched from a distance as troops of servants carried furniture and rolls of material into the Grange, saw Joseph sally forth to his prayer meetings and Mrs Dean about the house high on the moors, sometimes opening one of the lower windows, sometimes going into the bit of garden to fill a basket with twigs blown down by the wind.

I saw the girl Cathy too, she begotten of a summer loving between Catherine Earnshaw and Edgar Linton. She was certainly very pretty, delicately made with a high bosom and small neat features, her fair ringlets clustering on her shoulders, her eyes dark as her mother's had been.

She had a high sweet voice and used it mainly, as far I could tell, in issuing instructions to whoever was with her. Usually that was Mrs Dean who seemed content to do her bidding, which was not so surprising as she had taken charge of her since babyhood.

I saw Hareton once or twice but always in the distance. He seemed to spend a considerable portion of his time in carrying piles of books from one spot to another and twice I saw him put down his burden and turn to embrace her.

Then one afternoon, having ridden out to beneath Penistone Crags, I found him alone. Earlier I had seen the girl with Mrs Dean walking behind her, take the path towards Thrushcross Grange. The girl rode and led two packhorses with bulging parcels strapped to them and I guessed that more refurbishment of the Grange was about to take place. The girl was happily feathering her nest.

I had watched Joseph stump away earlier and I waited until the other two were out of sight before I remounted Minty and rode up the lower slopes towards that great house guarded by its naked gargoyles and flanked by its walled courtyard.

When I reached the courtyard I saw that Hareton Earnshaw had just emerged from the house though whether he had seen me coming or not I never enquired. Instead I dismounted and raised my voice a little.

'Forgive me but I wondered if the master of the house was at home?'

He answered obviously without thinking.

'I'm afraid Mr Heathcliff died several months ago.'

'Then you are the master now?' I pursued.

'I suppose so.'

For a moment he looked unsure and then he remembered his manners and came to the gate to unlatch it.

'I wished to make some enquiries,' I began.

He had taken Minty's rein and was leading her in. The pony had already nuzzled him in sign of recognition and he stroked her nose and said, his own head partly averted, 'Perhaps you would like to step indoors, Miss. . . ?'

'Stewart. Aspen Stewart,' I told him.

I wondered if Mrs Dean had mentioned her two interviews with me but evidently she had not, perhaps fearful of being accused of gossiping, for he answered at once, 'I'm pleased to meet you, Miss Stewart. You must be the lady who hired Minty for a spell.'

'I'm staying at the inn over in Gimmerton,' I informed him. 'If I might. . . ?'

'Yes, of course! Please do go in,' he said hastily. 'I'll just tether Minty here. I helped raise her so she knows me well.'

The main door was ajar. I went into the huge, high apartment where I had sat before and waited until he rejoined me, carefully scraping his boots on the iron grid before entering.

'And you are?'

'Hareton Earnshaw. Won't you sit down for a spell?'

He had pulled out one of the chairs and, in so doing, knocked the corner of the table where a pile of books rested, balanced rather untidily one upon the other. A couple fell to the floor and I bent swiftly to retrieve them.

'Thank you, miss.' He took them from me hastily and put them back on the table. There was something endearing in his slight clumsiness as if he was a creature more at home in the open spaces. 'Please sit down. If it's a business matter then it'll be Cath . . . Mrs Heathcliff you'll need to consult.'

'She is the owner?'

'Not exactly, miss.' He hesitated before drawing out another chair, this time without mishap, and seating himself on it. 'When Mr Heathcliff died Wuthering Heights reverted to me as Thrushcross Grange – over in the valley – reverted to Cath . . . to Mrs Heathcliff. But she generally handles any business matters pertaining to both properties. She has a good head for figures.'

'But you are the great reader here?'

I indicated the books.

'Only in the past few months,' he said, colouring slightly. 'I never had much time for education before. Mr Heathcliff depended on me for much of the work on the farm.'

'That sounds like a lot of work,' I said lightly.

'Oh no,' he hastened to explain. 'You see he worked himself just as hard and when he had to go away on business he trusted me to be in sole charge of the animals.'

'Was Mr Heathcliff related to you?' I asked.

'Not by blood, miss, but my father Hindley Earnshaw died when I were . . . was a little lad and Mr Heathcliff brought me up here. He was foster brother to my father.'

'He seems to have behaved well towards you then.'

'Oh yes, miss. He always treated me fairly. There were some who said he'd cheated me out of this place but the truth is that my father lost the property to him through gambling so it was very good of Mr Heathcliff to keep me on at all. He always treated me fairly.'

'Then it must be Mrs Heathcliff whom I must see about renting Thrushcross Grange,' I said.

'Renting the Grange?' His brow creased slightly and he pushed back his heavy dark hair in perplexity. 'Thrushcross Grange belongs to Mrs Heathcliff now and I know for a fact that she won't be renting it out. You see she wed her cousin, Mr Heathcliff's son, and when Linton died he left the Grange to his father and when Mr Heathcliff died it reverted to her. We are all cousins, miss, she being the daughter of the late Catherine Linton who was Mr Hindley's sister.'

'It all sounds quite confusing,' I said. 'Why will she not rent out the Grange?'

'Catherine and I are to be married on New Year's Day,' he said, his blush deepening. 'She . . . we have decided to live there and take Mrs Dean, Catherine's old nurse and housekeeper, though she'd not thank me for calling her old, with us.'

'Then I'm disappointed,' I said. 'I came into this neighbourhood for what was intended to be a brief sojourn but business keeps me here longer than I expected and lodging at an inn is a wearisome affair. I would be willing to pay double rent for a couple of months and if you need references then my lawyer—'

'Oh, I'm sure that wouldn't be necessary,' he broke in. 'If it were up to me then you'd be welcome to rent but until our marriage the Grange is her sole property.'

'And you look forward to living there?'

'Oh, anywhere Catherine wishes to live will suit me,' he said simply, 'though I've a fondness for this old place where I was born.'

'I can understand that,' I said with sympathy. 'This house does rather draw the eye with its carvings, and your name over the portal.'

'Oh, that Hareton Earnshaw lived three hundred years ago,' he told me. 'You know it's not very long since I couldn't read that nor much else if the truth be told.'

'You didn't go to school?'

'My father died when I were . . . was small and Mr Heathcliff cared for me. He hadn't much time for book-learning and there was always something to be doing on the farm. He taught me a lot did Mr Heathcliff, how to fish and shoot and deliver younglings and tell when a piece of ground was fertile and how to know when rain was on its way even though the sky showed blue.'

'And Mrs Heathcliff, your betrothed, prefers her old home at the Grange? That's very natural.'

'Aye she does,' he said. 'As you say it's only natural and she had a sad time when Mr Heathcliff brought her here for first her father and then her husband died, and Mr Heathcliff wasn't always as kindly with her as he might have been; he and her father were never on good terms and Mr Heathcliff could be rough when maybe he weren't meaning to be. But he was a good man at heart and I'd not hear a word said against him.'

'Of course you would not!' I exclaimed warmly. 'However

this does not solve my present problem. If Mrs Heathcliff is the person to see then perhaps I might consult her about a very short-term rental.'

'She will be down at the Grange again tomorrow,' he told me. 'It'd be wiser if you went there yourself for she likes to make her own decisions does Catherine. I'd only irritate her by putting my oar in. Miss Stewart, I'm forgetting my manners as usual. Would you like a cup of tea?'

'No thank you,' I said. 'Perhaps a cup of water.'

'I can get you that,' he said at once. 'We've a pump in the back kitchen.'

'This is quite a large property too,' I remarked.

'Aye, that's true enough,' he agreed, looking pleased. 'Mind you, it's not been properly repaired for years and some of the upper rooms are in a sad state, but I've some happy memories of times here. Would you like to see some of the other rooms?'

'Indeed I would,' I said pleasantly, and rose from my seat.

There was only one room that interested me. Hareton however passed it by, opening other doors to show me some chambers rudely furnished with beds and cupboards, others used obviously as lumber rooms with grain spilling out of sacks of corn and maize and broken stools waiting to be mended.

'The structure's sound,' Hareton observed. 'It'll stand for a good while yet. Joseph is to stay here to caretake after Catherine and I are wed, maybe with a lad to keep him company.'

'And this room?' I had reached the door and opened it by dint of advancing a few paces in front him.

The room with the boxbed and the portrait leaning its face against the wall was empty. Nothing, it seemed, had been touched since my first clandestine visit.

'This was once a handsome room!' I said casually, stepping over the threshold.

'It were . . . was kept shut up for years,' Hareton said.

'Why?'

'I asked Mr Heathcliff once,' he admitted. 'He told me as how he and my Aunt Catherine – he always called her Cathy – shared the bed here until she was near thirteen and he about fourteen. He said as how it was warm and sweet in the half dark with the moonlight silvering the window and the old thorn tree tapping its branches against the panes. He told me they used to bundle together and whisper strange tales to each other and when he woke in the night he smelled the soft scent of her. But my father made him sleep in the stables or up in the garrets and after that he never slept so well. But it wasn't my father's fault. It was the Lintons who came over and read him a lecture on the proper disposal of his household.'

'Your Catherine's grandparents?' I said as if my grasp of the various relationships was something new and untried.

'Yes, but they acted for the best I daresay,' he said, looking suddenly uncomfortable.

'And the room remained unoccupied?'

'I believe my aunt slept here alone but I was just a baby then. This was my Aunt Catherine.'

He bent and turned the portrait around and the amber gleam in the dark eyes of the young woman portrayed caught and held the light.

'You have eyes exactly like her!' I exclaimed.

'So I've been told but I don't remember her at all. My Catherine has dark eyes too but not quite the same.'

'Your aunt's eyes were beautiful,' I said, and had the secret pleasure of seeing him colour up again before he put the portrait back in its lowly position.

'And then she wed Mr Edgar Linton?' I continued.

'Aye she did and bore my Catherine and died within a twelve-month,' he said. 'That was over at the Grange and we never met the people from the Grange afterwards for years.'

'Can you recall your own father?' I moved casually and sat down on the end of the bed.

His face coloured slightly.

'Bits and pieces,' he said reluctantly. 'He had a problem with the drinking. After he died, Mr Heathcliff took care of me.'

'I've heard he was a hard man.'

'Aye, but folk say that when a man's good at business and makes his own way in the world,' he said, frowning. 'He was always good to me, Miss Stewart. He tried to be a father to his own son but Linton were that nesh!'

'Nesh?'

'Weak and peevish,' he said. 'Couldn't eat the food we ate here, wanted a fire even in summer and whatever else Joseph always built up a good fire at all seasons! Had to have a bit of a parlour to himself for his study and a tutor riding over three days a week to instruct him, and that cost Mr Heathcliff a fair bit of brass! It's not a friendly thing to say but I weren't sorry when the young whelp died. He was wed to my Catherine by then and I was sorry on her account for she did have a fondness for him! Anyway, he died in one of the other rooms upstairs with only her at his side and when she came down at last she were starved so I tried to draw her nearer to the fire but she flared up and told me to lay off!'

'She wasn't your Catherine then?' I said.

'Nay, that came later,' he said. 'She wanted me to learn to read nicely and then – well, things grew from there.'

'And Mr Heathcliff didn't object?'

'He did at first. Later on seeing us friendly like he seemed not to notice so much. He were in a right queer mood in the last weeks of his life. Wouldn't eat hardly anything, went out for hours on the moors, had a smile on his face as if something wonderful were going to happen. I was fair fretted about him and I went out and tried to talk him into having a bite but he told me to let alone, so I did.'

'And he died in this room?'

'Aye, he did. Nelly found him, open-eyed and cold after a stormy night. He died all alone, Miss Stewart, with nobody to hold his hand or speak soft to him. It made my heart ache it truly did.'

There were tears brimming in the amber glinted eyes and his long dark lashes were beaded with them.

'He must've known that you were fond of him,' I said softly.

'I hope so, miss. Problem is there's nobody to talk with about him now. My Catherine cannot abide to have him mentioned and so he never is mentioned between us. Joseph and Nelly don't mention him that often and I were going to say that I never mention him to anyone else and here I am telling you all about him! It's an odd thing that! Like I've known you a good long time when the truth is you only came to ask if the Grange was for rent and that you'd have to settle with Catherine anyway!'

I rose from the bed and stepped over to him, putting a casual hand on his bare forearm as I said, 'I have not told you my business here in Gimmerton. My late grandfather was Ronald Stewart. He has a fair-sized estate in Ireland, in a place called Imdel. He and Mr Heathcliff were business partners and now there are legal matters to be arranged.'

'Mr Heathcliff often went away,' he said in a puzzled fashion, 'but he never said where. Someone had to stay in charge of the animals while he were gone and he was a private kind of man, liked to keep his affairs close. Did you ever meet him?'

'On the odd rare occasion. He was always very kind to me,' I said.

'There now!' He brushed the moisture from his lashes in a childishly unselfconscious gesture. 'I knew he had a kindly heart under his stern manner! And I'll tell thee something else, Miss

Stewart! Mr Edgar Linton weren't as noble as some folks make out. My father was his brother-in-law and he might have shown him a bit of comradeship, helped him out of his gambling troubles, even offered to have me over at the Grange – not that Mr Heathcliff would've parted easily with me for he was far too fond of me for that – but Mr Edgar never even offered, never invited me over to meet with my cousin.'

'And Mr Edgar's sister who wed Mr Heathcliff? Was she kind to you?' I asked.

'I remember her,' he said suddenly. 'She were fair-haired and dainty and Mr Heathcliff brought her back one night. They were wedded then and it was plain she didn't take to us all! I were nearly six years old and my father was still alive but I spent a fair piece of time with Joseph, and though he's a tiresome body with his preaching and sermonizing, he used to treat me properly, saw that I got fed and went to bed, and yet she never had a kind word for me or him. And I remember the night she left here and ran away to London too! Children do remember things. I was supposed to be asleep but I woke up and heard voices below and I crept to the head of the stairs and listened and peeped through the bannisters and saw. It was the night my Aunt Catherine was buried though I couldn't remember her at all but Joseph told me something bad had happened and then I heard Mr Heathcliff crying. It's a terrifying thing for a child to hear a grown-up sobbing. I could see the fireplace with the flames dancing there and I could see Mr Heathcliff sat there, and the tears shining as they ran down his face, and hear his weeping, and my Aunt Isabella was mocking him, Miss Stewart! She was telling him to go back to the grave and lie on it, some such words, and then my father who was very drunk joined in the abuse and all at once Mr Heathcliff leapt up and grabbed a carving knife and Aunt Isabella ran to the door, still laughing at his grief and he threw the knife. It grazed her neck just beneath her ear and my father stumbled up and tried to hit Mr Heathcliff and they were wrestling together and Aunt Isabella was gone. I got up and I went back to bed and my bed was very cold and I wanted to cry but I was too cold. Fancy my recalling all that after so long a time!'

He had been speaking almost to himself and then he looked full at me and shook his head slightly as if he were bewildered in a strange place and said, 'I cannot think why I told you all that. I cannot think why I remembered that from so long ago.'

'I am glad,' I said, more moved than I might show, 'that you were kindly treated by Mr Heathcliff. It seems a pity Mrs Heathcliff will not admit there is goodness even in the worst of us.'

'My Catherine cannot see it so,' he said. 'Miss Stewart, you found Mr Heathcliff kind, did you not?'

'Very kind. My grandfather reposed great confidence in him. Of course I was not privy to all their conversations but I do know that he told grandfather that he thought more highly of his foster nephew than of his son. He said he had plans to advance him.'

'There! I told Catherine that he'd've seen me right in the end!' he said, his fine dark eyes kindling. 'I knew he had plans for me. He used to hint as much often but she swears it was a ploy to keep me working for him.'

'Will she be glad to be set straight on the matter though?' I asked, seating myself again on the edge of the bed. 'She may prefer to be left with her prejudices.'

'Oh, I'll say nought to Catherine,' he assured me. 'She isn't a young lady to be set right on a subject where she had decided notions. When she first visited us here to see her cousin Linton she burst into tears when she heard that I was her cousin too. Stood there sobbing and saying I was a dirty great lout – she was part right for I'd just been mucking out the stables! And Nelly Dean who'd come to fetch her home to the Grange told her not to be so unkind but she went on crying as if my being her cousin was a personal insult.'

'I hope you stood up for yourself,' I said.

'To tell the truth I were sorry that I'd made her cry,' he said. 'There was a new puppy just whelped in the stables and I went and got him and put him in her hands as a gift like but she pushed him back at me and went on crying. It took years before she began too, well, see me clear.'

'And she must've known how it would annoy Mr Heathcliff,' I said.

'Aye, for a bit it did but he wasn't himself by then,' Hareton said. 'He seemed in a kind of dream. No, he was not himself at all.'

'Perhaps it would be better if I were to see Mrs Heathcliff about the possible renting of the Grange for a month or two?' I said, rising. 'If she habitually disagrees with you—'

'Oh, we agree on most things,' he said, 'but the Grange is her property now, and as I said she has a better head for figures than I ever had.'

'I'll return tomorrow,' I said. 'You have told me a most interesting story, Mr Hareton. I shall not, of course, repeat any of it nor mention my visit here. Perhaps it would be wiser not to speak of my visit here? She might think it unseemly.'

'There's nowt unseemly in a bit of talking,' he said. 'Oh! I see what you mean! Well, I'll make sure I don't tell her then if it frets you but she knows full well no other lass would ever look at me!'

'Tells you that often, does she?' I murmured.

I didn't note his response for I half turned towards the boxbed as I spoke.

I had left a slight indentation in the mattress where I had

seated myself to hear the tale. There was a second one there now, deeper and wider, and when I put out my hand and briefly touched it the heat seared my fingers.

FIFTEEN

When I rode over to the Heights on the following day I half expected that Hareton, part of whose charm lay for me in his transparent honesty, might have told his Catherine of my visit, but as I dismounted the young lady herself opened the door.

She was indeed pretty, I thought, with the neat features of the flaxen-haired girl who had cast no reflection in the glass of the portrait at Thrushcross Grange but with the dark eyes that were clearly a factor in the beauty of the Earnshaw family. She had evidently left off any mourning for her late father-in-law, if indeed she had ever donned any, and her light blue dress with its patterned sprigs of darker flowers had a springtime tone.

'Mrs Linton Heathcliff?' I said.

'Yes.'

She nodded briefly, her eyes evaluating and largely rejecting my appearance which was hardly surprising since I had coiled back my hair and wore my plainest grey outfit with a hat that shaded my eyes.

'My name is Aspen Stewart,' I said. 'I am over here from Ireland on some business. I have been staying at the inn in Gimmerton. Now as I find the business will take a little longer than I expected I am hoping to rent a private property for a month or six weeks. I have learnt that your own property,

Thrushcross Grange—'

'Is not for rent,' she broke in with scant concern for politeness. 'I am to remarry on New Year's Day and my husband and I will live at the Grange. Indeed it is now being prepared for that event.'

'And this dwelling?'

'Will be shut up with an old servant as caretaker.'

'Then that is indeed a great pity,' I said. 'I had thought to offer a good price.'

'How much?' she asked abruptly.

I named a handsome sum and saw a faint gleam in the dark eyes. She might be young but she had inherited the sound financial sense that had made the Lintons the wealthiest landowners in the district.

'You will require to ask the permission of your future husband perhaps,' I hazarded.

'Thrushcross Grange is mine,' she said haughtily. 'Hareton would not dream of interfering in my concerns.'

'Then I am sorry indeed you are not amenable to the notion of a short rental,' I said. 'I've been given to understand that the Grange has been newly renovated; in such a remote neighbourhood with the owners absent I would fear intruders but perhaps the servants—'

'At present only one or two sleep on the premises. I don't think anyone however would dare. . . .'

'I would have spoken to your future husband,' I said, praying that Hareton Earnshaw would not appear round the corner, 'but at the inn I was told it was highly unlikely that he would agree to renting it.'

'The Grange is my property,' she said sharply. 'Hareton has nothing to do yet with any arrangements concerning it.'

'In any case I apologize for having troubled you.'

I had my hand on the pony's rein when she said, 'What you

have said makes good sense, Miss Stewart. Come into the house for a moment.'

Turning, she led the way in, leaving me to follow her. I could hear Joseph's voice raised in a doleful hymn somewhere in the back premises and she crossed the great chamber to where the high-backed settle separated living quarters from domestic and called, 'Do stop that dreadful caterwauling, you old fool! It's enough to frighten the angels!'

An indignant muttering was all that I could hear in reply.

'He's getting worse,' she said with an impatient shrug as she walked back towards me. 'That man arrived with the Ark and will have to be shot before we're rid of him! Do you have references?'

'I expect one from my lawyer, Mr Alistair, in a few days time,' I told her. 'I am not expecting to use the whole house, merely a bedroom and powder closet and a couple of the rooms downstairs. Oh, and if there is a servant on the premises – cooking is not one of my talents. I also wish to hire Minty for a longer period.'

'That will be extra,' she said, seating herself at the table and drawing pen, inkstand and paper towards her. 'I will rent what you have specified until the middle of December. I trust that will suit you?'

'Very well,' I said. 'I shall be returning to Ireland before Christmas.'

Even as I uttered the words a hunger swelled in me for the days of soft rainy chill when the houses were hung with mistletoe and holly and grandfather had taken me to the Midnight Mass to please our Catholic neighbours and some of our servants, though also to please ourselves as we saw the thatched crib with the little painted figures and the bright star above and heard the strains of ancient carols. I thought too of Hugh Brunty, playing the fiddle for the 'Adestes Fideles' and Ellis with

177

a light scarf over her golden hair and the latest baby in her arms. As a child I had sometimes muddled her with the Holy Virgin.

'I believe this will serve. I shall make a copy now if you agree to the terms,' Catherine Heathcliff said, handing me the paper and indicating where I should sign.

The terms were fair though not generous. I signed my name and waited while she made the copy and signed it herself.

'When do you wish to move in?' she asked, giving one copy of the agreement to me and folding the other away into a shallow drawer in the dresser.

'As soon as I have the reference from my lawyer,' I said.

'Very well,' she nodded, dusting her slim hands together as if she was a child playing at grown-up matters. In fact there was a certain childishness about her altogether. She would be near to nineteen, I guessed, but her manner was that of a very young girl playing at being an adult.

I guessed that her faults would be childish ones too: petty spite if anyone offended her, a tendency to rule those about her and to get her own way by deceit rather than defiance.

'Am I to offer condolences to the death of your father-in-law?' I enquired as I rose.

She stared at me for a moment, then uttered a high peal of laughter in which was no mirth.

'Mr Heathcliff was a devil,' she said flatly. 'He came into the Earnshaw family from hell itself I believe and hopefully is now residing in the same quarter. He tricked me into marriage with his weakling son in order to gain possession of the Grange and he tried before ever I was born to steal my mother from my father. He kept me here like a prisoner after Linton died and destroyed many of my books and, oh, the satisfaction of knowing him dead almost cancelled out the misery he caused me.'

'And now you are to wed another cousin? He too must feel relief.'

'Oh, Hareton cannot or will not be brought to utter one word of blame against Mr Heathcliff,' she said with a scornful curl of her lip. 'He tried to set Hareton against me when he was alive though Hareton will not admit the truth of it. No, we are at odds over Mr Heathcliff, not that we quarrel about it now for Nelly Dean, our housekeeper here, told me how it hurt Hareton when ill was spoken of his idol and as I can find nothing good to say then we avoid the distasteful subject altogether. Anyway, Hareton loathes it when I get into a temper and as I love him above everything, I refrain from tormenting him these days.'

She smiled as she spoke and I was caught by its fugitive charm. She had, I speculated, more spirit than her Aunt Isabella who had taunted Mr Heathcliff when he wept for his lost Cathy, but I mused also that this second Catherine would soon grow claws if her wishes were thwarted. The neat, calm features that she had inherited from her father might in the appropriate circumstances be translated into the sort of demonic rage of which her mother seems to have been capable.

'I will bid you good day then,' I said politely, remounting Minty.

I wondered how much she would tell Hareton or Mrs Dean about my visit. I suspected not much and I guessed also that they would keep mute about their separate interviews with me. These people locked up together in whirlpools of conflicting emotions preferred talking to strangers than to one another.

A few days later the reply to my letter to Mr Alistair arrived, the bulky envelope containing the documents for which I had asked and a letter from my lawyer himself which I read with mounting irritation.

Dear Miss Stewart,

Your surmises regarding the legal position as to the owner-
ship of Wuthering Heights and Thrushcross Grange are
correct, the enclosed certificate of marriage proving this
point. I must however warn you most seriously as to the
wisdom of implementing your plans. Your grandfather left
you well provided with a possibility of increase as well as
the Stewart property. Since you were born and bred in
Ireland and can have no lasting affinity with either
Yorkshire or its inhabitants then I must again counsel you
to think seriously about your intentions which while
commensurate with the letter of the law, do, in my opinion,
conflict with the moral law.

The Brunty family, as usual, wish to be remembered to
you. Also Brigit, who waits for a letter from you.

Yours respectfully,

G. Alistair

My lawyer was obviously a man of honour where others were
concerned as well as myself I thought, and studied the enclosed
marriage certificate with interest.

As I had long suspected, the Dublin wedding had taken place
four months before my own birth.

Whether he had forced her or not, and I suspected he had
not, he had waited to lay claim to his pound of flesh before he
had agreed to wed my pretty, red-haired mother.

I sat in my room at the inn, musing over the people and
events that have shaped and moulded my life. And I began to
see plainly how the strong and the weak prey upon each other,
how the weak have their own strengths and the strong their own
weaknesses, so that each finds a mirror in a counterpart. And I

understood too that some had to die in order that the endings be fulfilled.

A few days later, I received a terse note to inform me that I might now take temporary possession of Thrushcross Grange. It was signed by Catherine Heathcliff and I looked long at the still childish script.

She had some trace of her dead mother's temper but she had been reared as a Linton in sheltered luxury. Had my grandfather lived then I too might have become a Catherine. And I was glad in that moment to admit to myself that his dying had prevented that and also that the rare visits of my father had tempered my silk with steel.

I paid the bill at the inn, arranged for my luggage to be taken to the Grange and, mounted on Minty, set off across the moors. It was misty that day and I held her in check lest she stumble into a bolthole.

I passed the gaunt outlines of the Heights and the high crags of Penistone and, as I rode, the mist thickened until the air was full of swirling shapes that formed themselves out of the clouds and drifted here and there as the still gentle wind breathed upon them.

When I came to the gates of the Grange I was surprised to find Hareton there alone waiting. He stood by his own horse, the damp mist curling the ends of his black hair and I reined in Minty and looked at him for almost a minute before his abstracted gaze withdrew from whatever had held his attention. Then he gave a hesitant smile and said, 'I thought as how someone should be here to welcome you.'

'You're very kind, Mr Earnshaw.'

He helped me to dismount, though I might have managed it perfectly well by myself, and for an instant glanced about as if he expected to see another person standing there. Then he said, 'I beg your pardon, Miss Stewart, but I'm not well used to being called Mr Earnshaw yet. Most people still call me Hareton.'

'But you and I are not on those terms of friendship,' I said playfully.

'It's just that when I hear Mr Earnshaw I half expect my father to walk around the corner,' he said, half embarrassed. 'Mr Heathcliff had only the one name to serve him and I weren't . . . wasn't called anything but Hareton while he was alive.'

'May I have that pleasure?' I asked as we went along the path. The ground was strewn thickly with leaves of scarlet and gold and bronze and we scuffed them with our boots as we went along.

'Yes, miss. Hareton sounds more friendly like,' he said.

'My name is Aspen,' I said.

'Is that an Irish name, Miss— Aspen? I never heard it before.'

'It was my grandfather's choice,' I lied. 'He was from the Highlands originally so I suppose it may have a Scottish connection.'

'I've never been out of Yorkshire,' he said.

'Do you want to travel?'

'Never thought about it, Mi— Aspen. Mr Heathcliff had been in foreign parts but he told me that Yorkshire was better than any. I never heard him speak of Ireland though.'

'Ireland is softer and greener than this,' I said. 'We have our hills and rocks though, but the weather is milder.'

'It's been pretty mild this year up to now,' he said.

'Yes. Yes, it has. Tell me, did Mrs Heathcliff say how she felt about letting Thrushcross Grange again?'

'That's her property,' he said, a slight withdrawal in his manner. 'She said as how she got a fair rental. I don't go interfering in her affairs.'

'Nor she in Wuthering Heights?'

I had put the question softly and for a moment I thought he

hadn't heard for he said nothing but walked along, still scuffing the leaves. Then he said abruptly as if the words had been dragged out of him, 'The truth is that I'm not educated enough to go into the ins and outs of property and rentals and such like. My Catherine says as some have the knack and some haven't. I like better to be with the animals but when we get to the Grange she's all kinds of plans for me being the gentleman like her father was, sitting as a magistrate and all that.'

'You will grow accustomed to it,' I said.

'Aye, perhaps.' He heaved an involuntary sigh as we turned in the direction of the stables and, after a moment, said in a more cheerful tone, 'I like reading fine though. There's a good library of books at the Grange and I shall work my way through them.'

'Will you have the leisure if you're sitting as magistrate?' I enquired artlessly.

'I cannot see myself on the bench!' he said and laughed.

'And respectable in a high stock and flowing cravat?'

'Lord, no!'

He flung back his head and laughed again, teeth white in his sunbrowned face, the sound joyful and spontaneous.

'Will you show me round the Grange?' I asked as he tethered the horses and poured water into the trough.

'Well, I'm not over familiar with it myself,' he admitted. 'I only come here when Catherine asks me to come. Of course it's my own fault for not trying harder to understand that it's her old home where she was born and her parents died and it holds all her happy memories. I never set foot in the place until Mr Heathcliff died.'

'Then I must go in alone and unwelcomed,' I said.

'Nay, miss! Aspen I mean,' He gave me a warm look. 'I'll come in and find out which rooms are for you. Catherine said something about notices pasted to the doors.'

We had left the stables and entered through the side door. As

I had twice taken that route before I had to remind myself that I was not in any position to march ahead and so betray my previous visits.

'That door should have been locked,' he said. 'The keys are kept up at the Heights save for a couple of spare ones the servants use when they come to clean and sweep. This here is the kitchen. And this must be the room she set aside for your living.'

He pointed to a notice fixed to double doors and I followed him with a private sinking of my heart into the long apartment with the portrait of Edgar Linton and the long windows at the far end reaching to the floor. Everything was polished and shining now, dustcovers removed from the sofas and armchairs, the long oak table on which the first Catherine's body had lain bearing a vase filled with branches of hawthorn, the leaves discoloured and drooping.

'There doesn't seem to be anyone about,' Hareton said, going back to the door and raising his voice in a shout. 'Happen a couple of servants'll be about somewhere. And someone should've laid the fire and lit it! You being from a warmer clime you'll likely feel the cold more. Stay here while I find out what's going on.'

I sat down on one of the high-backed seats and waited until Hareton came in again.

'There's a woman doing laundry out back,' he said. 'I looked in the kitchen and there's food there for a meal, a cold joint and bread and some pie. I reckon Catherine got her dates muddled and expects you in the morning.'

'Then I must stay here alone.'

'At least I can get the fire going and make you a bit of supper,' he said.

'Won't Mrs Heathcliff expect you at the Heights?'

'Later maybe. She doesn't enquire after me when I'm out in

the fields. I'll get this fire going.'

He was busy with coal and some small logs and a tinderbox. I took off my cloak and hat and sat down to watch him.

There was a sudden flare of the wood and paper he was holding before the newborn fire and he uttered an exclamation of pain as the blaze caught the sleeve of the rough tunic he wore over his breeches.

'My God! you're on fire!'

I leapt up and banged his arm with the flat of my hand and the flame spluttered and died, leaving a charred stain and himself still on one knee, his face contorted with pain.

'Don't move! I'll get this off!'

I dragged the tunic over this head and saw the angry scorch-marks on his upper arm.

'Stay still. I'll get something for it!'

I ran through to the kitchen and the back premises beyond but the laundry woman had gone. I poured water into a bowl, grabbed at a large slab of butter and some clean cloths drying over a cold range and hurried back to where he still knelt, nursing his injured arm.

'Come, sit on one of the chairs,' I urged. 'I will tend this for you lest it blister.'

Somehow or other I got him into the armchair and knelt to dab the burn with cold water and sear on the butter. It was a painful but not a bad burn and he hardly winced as I tore the cloths into strips and bound them about his upper arm. Indeed he seemed to be in a kind of dream, his eyes unfocused.

'You must sit quiet for a spell,' I said. 'I am going to light the fire again and make us some tea. Tea is very good for shock.'

'Yes,' he said and went on staring into his private dream.

I relit the fire and watched it blaze up and brought in a kettle of water and the wherewithal for brewing tea from the kitchen.

While it was heating on the hob I returned to his side,

smoothing the tense muscles of his back with my fingers, feeling him gradually relax though his gaze remained abstracted.

'Come drink,' I urged, pouring tea and adding a spoonful of sugar. Milk I had been unable to find.

He drank obediently when I held the cup to his lips, his colour gradually returning.

'That was a near escape,' I said, taking the cup away and pushing the long hair from his forehead. 'The burn should be properly dressed. Will Mrs Heathcliff know what to do or shall I ride for a doctor?'

'Nay, it'll mend itself soon enough,' he said.

'But you must eat something before you go. I shall get the meat and the bread,' I tempted.

'I'm not hungry,' he said indifferently.

I went and got the food anyway and made him swallow a few pieces of the meat, and then he began to shiver as if the fire had never been lit at all.

'Hareton, what ails you?'

I sat on the arm of the chair and pulled him towards me, his uninjured arm going about my waist as he leaned against me.

'I cannot tell,' he said at last, his voice hoarse. 'Did you see. . . ? No, you would have said . . . did you feel. . . ?'

'See what? Feel what?' I demanded.

'I was pushed,' Hareton said. 'I was pushed towards the blaze and it flared up my sleeve and I couldn't—'

'I was nowhere near you!' I said.

'No, it wasn't you!' He shuddered again but there was more joy than terror in his face.

'By what? By whom?'

'I don't know,' he said, leaning his head against me as if I were part of the chair. 'I saw a hand out of the corner of my eye. It bore a ring on the smallest finger, a ring of dried grey bones. I wish I could remember where I've seen that ring before.'

SIXTEEN

When he had gone, having wisely decided to say nothing to Catherine about his visit to the Grange or the mishap he had suffered, the fire blazed merrily now with no sign of disturbance though it failed to warm the huge apartment. Even though, as twilight stole on, I lit several candles and two lanterns, I found that as well as being cold the room was even bigger than it appeared to be, with sharp corners where gloom lingered and a ceiling whose high mouldings assumed different angles every time one glanced at them. I took one of the lanterns and prowled through the other chambers, finding a notice signifying tenancy on the door of the bedroom where I had found the letter. When I looked again in the little secret drawer I saw the letter was still there though it had come loose from its moorings and hung down awkwardly.

Isabella Linton had fancied herself in love with Mr Heathcliff, had defied her brother in order to elope with him, yet must have known even as she prepared for her flight that her feelings deceived her, that she embarked on a heartbreak course and within a few months would have fled south.

Mr Heathcliff had used her pliant affection but not bothered to keep up the pretence on his side. That had been cruel of him but when had he not been cruel in his dealings with other people? And it was Isabella who had taunted him when he had wept for his Cathy.

I left exploration of the rest of the house until daylight and, though I found my luggage neatly stacked in a rear passage, I left it there. Wrapping myself in my cloak, I lay down on the sofa before the fire and slept fitfully among the lighted candles like a virgin on some pagan altar.

The morning brought Mrs Dean, tapping at the lattice and making me start up in alarm.

'Miss Stewart! what a mess and a muddle!' were her first words when I opened the long windows to admit her. 'A lad from the inn came by to say your things had been sent here and then Mrs Heathcliff recalled that you had mentioned you might move in yesterday and by then it was too late to come over and so I'm here to set things to rights and . . . you slept on the sofa here?'

We had paused for a moment in our bustle and she stared at the crumpled cushions and the ashes in the grate in dismay.

'I was very comfortable,' I said. 'If Mrs Heathcliff thinks to drive me out of her old home after one night and then refuse to give me my money back she is sadly mistaken.'

'My Miss Catherine isn't like that!' Indignation quivered in her plump face. 'She was always a sweet little girl – Mr Edgar doted on her and she thought the sun, moon and stars of him. She would never harm or hurt anything willingly!'

'I thought she insulted Hareton Earnshaw,' I said.

'Did I mention that? Well, she was put out to find a farmhand who couldn't read or write was her first cousin and that's only natural, for Mr Edgar brought her up like a lady in ignorance of the Earnshaws. And of course when she first visited the Heights and met Hareton she was thick with Linton – Mr Heathcliff's son if you recall my saying.'

'Whom Mr Heathcliff forced her to marry.'

'Well, by then she'd started to realize that her little romance was no more than a girlish whim,' Mrs Dean excused. 'Linton had a bad nature, Miss Stewart, there's no denying it, but Catherine thought it a gentle one and was sadly distressed when it proved otherwise. Anyway that's all past for she loves Hareton now and soon they'll be living here and I shall feel at home once more; since Mr Heathcliff died I haven't felt easy in the old house. Now, let's get your bags unpacked and here are the two servants who will wait upon you and I believe Catherine said that Miss Isabella's room was most comfortable and convenient during your tenure.'

From then on she was in her element, instructing the two women who had arrived with news of a stableboy also on his way, making a list of provisions that must be brought from the village, checking the woodshed, rooting about in a large linen cupboard to find bedcovers. It was plain that yesterday wouldn't have been too soon for her to resume her duties as housekeeper.

'I think,' she said at last, coming back into the large apartment, 'that everything's in good order now. This was one of Mrs Linton's favourite rooms. She and Mr Edgar – that's his portrait on the wall – used often to sit here in the late afternoon and watch the birds fluttering in the trees and he would lean out and pluck an apple or a pear for her. After she became ill he had the whole room fitted out for her as a downstairs bedroom and as she grew stronger she used to lie most of the day on that sofa, just dreaming her hours away. She was never quite the same after the brain fever took her, gentler and quieter. Mind, my Miss Catherine was well on the way by then and we were all fearful of upsetting her. I wonder now if her last meeting with Mr Heathcliff didn't undo all the progress she'd made; they were at each other like two animals, if animals ever weep and embrace. Of course Miss Catherine knows nothing of this.'

'Did she die in this room?' I asked.

'No, in her old chamber upstairs where she was first taken ill,' Mrs Dean assured me. 'She was laid out here and poor Mr Edgar watched by her for so long that he grew faint and had to retire and while he was gone . . . aye, it's a sad story. But Miss Catherine brought joy into this house again when she was born and apart from a few little naughtinesses she was always a bidd-able child.'

'And she loved Linton,' I murmured.

'Oh, a girlish romance such as most of us have! He was a nice looking boy, fair with none of his father's darkness but he was spoilt and selfish and she soon found that out. His death was no great loss. Now is there anything else you need before I go?'

'I think I shall be well served here,' I said.

'And I'm sorry again that Miss Catherine . . . I ought to say Mrs Heathcliff, which she still is until she becomes Mrs Earnshaw but she'll always be my Miss Catherine to me. Hareton ought to think himself the most favoured being on earth that she chose him. He would have come over himself by the by but he went over to Gimmerton to get his shoulder checked out. He'd a bit of an accident with his fowling piece, oh, months ago, before Mr Heathcliff died, and it still pains him now and then. Well, he'll be quite the young gentleman soon and all Mr Heathcliff's plans to turn him into a yokel will be finally set at nought. Good day, Miss Stewart.'

She took her buxom self off and I went up to wash and change into a different dress, combed my hair into a semblance of neatness and slipped the bone ring on my finger.

Where Hareton Earnshaw was concerned I was becoming as acute as a homing pigeon and when I had bypassed the orchard and reached the shrubberies and the grassy lawns beyond I saw him, walking rapidly up and down as if unsure what direction to take.

'Hareton, are you better? Did Mrs Heathcliff lose her temper when you were late?' I exclaimed, hurrying towards him.

'Nay, she said nothing,' he said. 'She did mention at breakfast that she thought you were moving in today. Anyway she said you must come to tea sometime, when it suited you.'

'That was very kind of her,' I said. 'How is your arm?'

'No more than a bit of soreness left.' He eyed me shyly for a moment, then said abruptly, 'what I said last evening about, well about the hand, I cannot think why I thought I saw anything.'

'But you recall the ring?'

'Aye, made of tiny, brittle bones, small enough for a lady's finger—'

He stopped dead and stared at the bare hand I had just extended to him.

'Mine was not the hand that pushed you,' I said. 'I was too far away.'

'But the ring?' He looked so confused that I longed to put my arms about him and hold him tightly.

'Mr Heathcliff gave it to me,' I said. 'On one of his trips to Ireland to discuss business with my grandfather, he gave me this ring.'

'That was when I saw it!' Hareton suddenly declared. 'No, not in Ireland for I've never been out of Gimmerton, but on Mr Heathcliff's finger. I must've been just a little lad and I saw the ring and asked him about it and he turned away without answering and I never saw it again until . . . Miss Aspen, I don't understand what's happening. Mr Heathcliff had a gruff manner but he never raised his hand to me so why would he . . . but he's dead! I closed his eyes and kept him company until they buried him.'

'Mrs Dean said he died with a terrible grimace on his face,' I said.

'That he did not!' His colour rose and he answered energetically. 'He had a gladsome look on his face, and he looked younger than I had ever seen him look, not that he was old for he hadn't reached forty! But he did sometimes appear grim and silent and he could be harsh. But he looked as if he'd just been given his heart's desire. Mrs Dean is a good sort and always kind to me, she it was persuaded Catherine to be polite and not scorn me, but she had a downer on Mr Heathcliff after he came back into Yorkshire and started visiting here. She liked this house better than the Heights. She said it were . . . was more than a gentleman's residence. It might have belonged to a knight of the realm one day if Mr Edgar hadn't shut himself away grieving in his study.'

'She will be pleased to leave the Heights then,' I said.

We had begun to walk along one of the bridle paths and overhead the trees swayed gently in the breeze.

'Aye, she says as she feels that Mr Heathcliff is still about the place,' he said. 'She feels he's watching her though why he should I can't think. And a few people from the village have said they've passed our house and seen him and his Cathy – that was what he always called my aunt – looking out of that upstairs window in that bedchamber I showed you. I never told Catherine about that visit. I'd not want her to think I go showing strangers over the house.'

'You showed me,' I said. 'I was a stranger.'

'Aye, I suppose you were.' He turned his head slightly and gave me one of his hesitant, heartbreaking smiles. 'You know, Miss—'

'Aspen,' I said.

'Aspen. You know I never thought of you as a stranger at all after the first few minutes. It was as if I'd always known you, always had the shadow of you across my mind, as if – this is going to sound clean daft and if it offends you why I'll walk away and there's an end on it, but when I felt miserable, and I sometimes did when Mr Heathcliff went away on business, I used to draw a picture in my mind of another self inside me and it weren't a lad but a girl with long black hair glinted with red and dark deep eyes like Mr Heathcliff himself, and that was comforting but sad. I never could figure even in dreams how to bring the little girl out and have her bear me company.'

'I have always wished for company too,' I said, and took his hand as we walked, feeling the roughness at the base of the fingers where he had held scythe or hoe, the long fingers themselves and the broad palm with the warm skin pressed against my own palm. 'When I visited your home I felt as if I too had arrived in a place where I had never been but knew more intimately than even my grandfather's house in Ireland. Your home is a grand old building, full of echoes and warmth and the memory of spices and I can understand your not wanting to leave it for this chilly, grand place shut away from the Heights and Penistone Crags.'

'Have you been up on the summit of the crags?' he asked.

I shook my head. 'It must be wonderful up there when the sun's out,' I said.

'Aye, it is. There's a bit of a cave near the top, folk call it the fairy cave, and in summer when the sun gilds the crags long ribbons of sunlight flow like water under the arched roof and one can hear birds singing even when there are no birds about. I went up there once and an old woman was seated in the cave, with long grey plaits and little apples at the ends of her plaits, and she looked at me and said nowt and I stood there like a fool and just as I was about to say I thought as how I knew her from where dreams come, she laughed and her laugh echoed like bells all round the cave and I turned and stumbled down to the level ground again. I've never told anyone that before.'

'I too have seen the woman,' I said.

'Anyway I never said owt to anyone or they might say I'd been at my father's brandy bottle,' he said.

'Not even Mrs Heathcliff?'

I withdrew my hand as I spoke and glimpsed his fingers make a little groping movement as if they were lonely.

'No, Catherine would think I was trying to scare her,' he said. 'She loves the crags of course because they look so pretty when the sun shines but she doesn't like queer, unexplained things. She likes to be up and about and enjoying life.'

'And instructing you in the art of being a gentleman,' I said lightly.

'Aye, she's her heart set on that,' he said.

'And she loves you more than she loved her first husband, Linton?'

'She was more sorry for him, you know,' he said. 'He was fair like her and slender and felt the cold and fretted if things weren't quite right and she liked to make him comfortable and all.'

'As she liked to make you comfortable when she decided to be your friend?'

'Well,' he said, his tone suddenly uneasy. 'I reckon she won't feel comfortable herself until we're out of the Heights and over here. She and Mrs Dean are going out to buy wedding stuff in a day or two. All the very best for she wants a grand wedding with the neighbours invited and a party afterwards. I'm not to see anything until the day. They're going over to Leeds to get the finest silk for the dress and the bonnet and lace for the veil.'

'I would like if I ever wed to slip away very quietly,' I said, 'and wear something simple and pretty and afterwards steal away with my bridegroom and find some grassy hollow and pleasure him until the dawn lit the sky.'

'They're planning on spending the night in Leeds,' he said.

For a moment we looked at each other and then he turned

and walked away rapidly as I stood there with the trees creaking and rustling overhead. I could hear a bird singing loudly from some nearby tree though it was not the season for mating.

SEVENTEEN

Catherine arrived the following day, apologizing prettily for having muddled her days.

'Everything was arranged in such a rush,' she said. 'As I had no intention in the beginning of renting out Thrushcross Grange again, my own decision took me by surprise. Mr Heathcliff rented it out over a year ago but had ill-luck with his tenant there, for Mr Lockwood came floundering up to the Heights on two or three occasions and made an utter fool of himself, mistaking me for Mr Heathcliff's wife and then for Hareton's. At that time I was not in the least friendly with my cousin and he felt equal scorn for me, and poor stupid Mr Lockwood became tongue-tied and upset the dogs by making faces at them. I had not laughed so much in a long time! And then he caught a chill and was confined to his room for weeks and finally went south again.'

'Without returning?' I said.

'Oh, he came back to pay off the rest of his rental last month sometime,' she said. 'I did not see him but Nelly told him about Mr Heathcliff's strange death. Hareton and I didn't see him. We had taken a ride by moonlight if I remember rightly.'

'And you are to be married soon,' I said.

'On New Year's Day, and then we will reside here at the

196

Grange. Wuthering Heights is to be shut up and left to decay, which is the best fate I can devise for such a hell-hole. I have been more miserable in that den than anywhere else in my life, Miss Stewart! If you knew the whole story you would pity me!'

'I understand you married your other cousin there,' I said.

'Linton, yes. I suppose the villagers have been gossiping. Oh, I imagined myself in love with him for a long time, you know, for he was fair and blue-eyed and could be charming company when he was in a good mood, but his ill health made him tiresome. I cannot abide ill people for very long.'

She herself looked the picture of good health, her cheeks pink and her fair ringlets bouncing on her shoulders. Surely a true Linton, I thought, save for the dark eyes of the Earnshaws. I thought too that she had probably inherited some of the wayward tempers of her mother as well as the superior airs of her father.

'Nelly and I travel to Leeds tomorrow to buy materials for the wedding gown and trousseau,' she was rattling on. 'I cannot wear white since I am a widow so I shall wear blue, I think, or gold of a paler shade than my hair, and I am determined upon a veil! We shall have a grand time and though Hareton doesn't yet know it, I am having a suit of black broadcloth made for him too. Mr Heathcliff deliberately kept him ignorant because he hated his father so greatly but I am determined to raise him up.'

'Will he enjoy that?' I ventured to ask.

'Hareton is always anxious to please me these days,' she said, turning at the door to shake hands again. 'He used not to like me at all but matters are altered now.'

She mounted her pony, her long pink-lined cape floating behind her, and trotted off down the drive.

I thought then that she was like a little girl with a toy but what she would do when she grew weary of playing with it as she had with Linton I had no notion.

I had, in any case, other things on my mind. The proof of my parents' marriage altered everything, for the two houses had only reverted to their proper heirs in default of Mr Heathcliff's having had no relatives closer than a daughter-in-law and a foster nephew. Also, I reminded myself, in default of his having not made a will before his death. That was surprising to me because my father had always been spoken of, if never with affection, at least as a man of good business sense.

Now, though nobody else knew it, I could claim both properties. I had a pleasant vision of Catherine renting Thrushcross Grange from me and then my thoughts grew grave again for, whether she inherited or rented, the plain fact remained that she would marry Hareton Earnshaw.

I could not, still cannot, understand myself. I had gained the age of twenty-one and been sufficient unto myself during that time, not taking covert glances at any of the young men in Imdel, happy to be my own mistress with rare visits from Mr Heathcliff to both disturb and enliven me. Now, without knowing how or why, my mind was thronged with Haretons. They appeared in scene after imagined scene, Hareton washing in the beck, Hareton stroking Minty's nose as he greeted me at the Heights, Hareton with his head leaning against me as he winced with pain after the beringed hand had sent him spinning into the fire, Hareton walking with me down the bridle path with our palms touching, warming, tingling – and other scenes not yet enacted but spiralling in my imagination.

I cared and still care nothing for the cold, elegant house with its surrounding parkland where the late Edgar Linton stares down impassively from the walls, and the pale Isabella drifts like cobwebs, leaving no reflection.

Yet when I thought of the Heights I saw it not with its burden of tragedy but as it once must have been with Mr Heathcliff and his Cathy still childlike, and Hindley away at College and

Mrs Dean a buxom young woman with links to the family perhaps even nearer than she suspected. And that house could be made so again and its ghosts appeased.

The next day I waited until the pony-trap which could convey Catherine and Mrs Dean to the Leeds coach had gone past the high crags of Penistone and then I continued on my own way, riding Minty, wearing the apple earrings with a simple grey habit, the little box with the ring of bones in it safely in my pocket.

Hareton was waiting and pretending not to wait, his eyes intent on examining the wall for imaginary cracks, his hands plucking at the odd sprig of herb as if his future depended on it.

'Good afternoon!' I called when I was within earshot and he cleared the low wall and ran the few yards towards me long-legged, a smile of pure pleasure on his face.

'Aspen, I hoped you'd visit!'

His voice was warm and deep, only the slightest harshness of the north discernible in its timbre, and his amber-glinted dark eyes between their long black lashes smiled at me even as his lips uttered the greeting.

'It's lonely at the Grange,' I confided. 'At least at the inn there were other guests moving in and out and the staff there who were very civil.'

'But the rooms Catherine chose are comfortable?' He spoke rather anxiously as if he genuinely wanted my stay to be a pleasant one.

'Oh yes,' I said, letting him help me to dismount. 'I am sure she could not have known that your aunt, Catherine, was laid out in the sitting-room or that my bedroom belonged once to Isabella Linton whose marriage to Mr Heathcliff proved so unhappy.'

'I am sure she did not,' he said, but the slight frown with

which his brow was marked as he led Minty into the stable made me wonder if the present Catherine were given to playing mocking little tricks.

The huge apartment was warm, cosy despite its size and swept clean with the platters and jugs on the high dresser gleaming. Under its arch a pair of puppies suckled their dam contentedly. On the table in a blue bowl some sprigs of late heather had been placed in water though their colour was already fading.

'For Mr Heathcliff,' Hareton said, noting the direction of my glance. 'He were fond of heather and harebells, said they were more honest than cultivated flowers.'

'You put flowers on his grave?'

'No, he'd not want that and Catherine would fly into a tantrum if she thought I ever went near,' he said. 'No, they're for my own looking. The truth is that while I'm not much of a gardener – Catherine likes those pretty little beds with pinks and Spanish poppies in them – I like to see things growing wild. In the summer the moors are like carpets of golden gorse and purple heather as if the sky and the coming of thunder married together above the grass. In winter the snow generally covers everything of course, but one can always find a sprig of something here and there. If I lie dying in winter I hope someone finds a sprig of late heather to put beside me before I leave.'

For an instant I was too moved to speak, and in that instant I felt as if the Heights itself was turning into ice that would melt into nothing with the coming of spring and that Hareton and I would blend into the snowflakes, cold circling cold in a white world.

'Why do you talk of dying?' I said sharply. 'You are not ill?'

'I was never in better health,' he said. 'I don't know what made me say that. Did I frighten you?'

'For a moment,' I admitted truthfully, and he put his hand on mine and ushered me to a chair near the blazing fire.

'I'm that sorry!' He had knelt to chafe my hands in his own. 'Thoughtless like! Catherine is always trying to get me to mend my manners and I as often forget! I've made a pot of tea. Would you like some?'

'Yes indeed I would. You're very kind,' I said.

'Well, loving kindness never did any harm,' he said, rising to pour the tea.

'And no person rejects it,' I said, untying the ribbons of my cape.

'Some do,' he muttered and, for a moment, looked rough and surly.

'From you?'

'Aye well, it were a few months back and then some and I've almost forgotten it,' he said.

'Almost?'

'Not really,' he said, somewhat sheepishly. 'I mean I don't hold any grudges. It were when Linton died. Poor Catherine had a time of it for she'd grown to hate him by then – at the start the pair of them liked to make game of me, my bad grammar and my accent – but anyway, Linton died and Catherine stayed upstairs for above two weeks after that. Nelly Dean was at the Grange then and wasn't suffered to visit here. Zillah took Catherine her food up and tried to be friendly but never got any road with that, and when Catherine did come down she looked starved with cold. I offered to let her sit by the fire to warm herself – she were like a little cat that spits at everything, and she turned on me and said she'd rather freeze to death out of doors than have my disagreeable voice in her ear. Of course she was moithered and all that but her words did hurt. Months went by before she started to put up with me being around, even Zillah was gone by then and Mrs Dean come and I suppose Catherine felt sorry that she hadn't been more friendly. But she was too unhappy, under the circumstances I never really blamed her. Anyway she started being willing to make friends about a month before Mr Heathcliff died. He noticed and he didn't much like it because he reckoned she were trying to turn me against him, and that he'd never stand! He were fond of me and I of him. Anyways, soon after he died and soon after that . . . she never meant to hurt me.'

'Words can hurt,' I said gently and let my hand lie on his.

'Aye, but I was a fool to take notice,' he said.

He had lifted my hand and was caressing it with his long fingers as if hardly aware of what he did.

'And now you love her,' I said.

'Aye, I do.'

'And like her?'

He jerked his head upwards and stared at me.

'Like?' he repeated.

'When passion dies and there's no liking then there's nothing.' I was thinking of Hugh Brunty drawing his wife's face in his mind as he leant on one elbow to watch her sleeping.

'I reckon liking's important,' he said slowly, rising and taking the other chair, 'but passion doesn't always die. Mr Heathcliff loved one woman all his life as if they were part of each other.'

'And now they rest together.'

'I don't know about rest. I'm none so sure about that!' He had poured the tea but both our cups remained neglected on the table between us. 'There are folk who say they've seen them, sometimes on the moors and sometimes up on Penistone Crags and once or twice looking out of the upper window.'

'Have you seen them yourself?' I asked.

'Nay, and I'd not be frightened if I did,' he said with a slight smile. 'I reckon as they'll rest when their selves are satisfied or until whatever's not done gets done. If I knew it were owt like that I'd try to get it done for them to give them a bit of peace, but I've never seen them. Have you?'

'Glimpses,' I admitted slowly. 'But then perhaps all houses are haunted even by the living.'

'Joseph would say that's blasphemy,' he said with another smile.

'Where is Joseph today?' I asked abruptly.

'Taken some cattle over to the Leas and plans to spend the night with a preacher friend.'

'I see.'

I smiled myself, letting the mischief linger in my eyes and at the corners of my mouth.

'I don't know why,' Hareton said, 'but when I see you I see a kind of image of myself. It sounds stupid but when you're around it's as if Mr Heathcliff were saying, "there's unfinished business, lad." I know I sound as if I'm mizzled.'

'I don't think you're ... mizzled? What a lovely word! Mizzled. No, I don't think that,' I said and leaned to recapture his hand. 'I do believe that Mr Heathcliff had plans for you but he was interrupted by his own dying. I do think he had very definite plans for you.'

'He never mentioned what to you or your grandfather?'

'Only very obscurely. I hardly ever met him.'

'He used to say that I reminded him of himself,' Hareton said. 'Before he got himself educated I mean. Catherine says he kept me down because he hated my father who mistreated him, but I think he saw himself as a lad in me, and he didn't want me turning into a spoilt brat like Linton or a nose in the air landowner like Mr Edgar.'

'Did you know, Hareton,' I said softly, 'that you are a truly pleasant person?'

'Well, I try to do right by folks,' he said, colouring up as he spoke.

'And by yourself too, I hope?'

203

'As to that I never figured I were worth that much,' he said after a moment. 'Anyway Mr Heathcliff liked me well enough as I was and so did Joseph come to that. Joseph's a bit mad but not a bad old stick.'

'And Catherine would call you her rough diamond,' I said.

'She probably would.' He rose and went to poke the fire, his long lean back with the broad shoulders curving away from me. I tasted desire in my throat.

'Do diamonds relish being polished?' I asked softly.

'Maybe yes, maybe no.' He straightened up and turned round. 'I'll be plain with you though I don't reckon you're being plain with me. Catherine loved Linton for a long time until she saw his faults and when he wouldn't mend them at her bidding, she hated him. She hated me for a long while but when I started to speak softer and pay heed then she began to love me, and we're to wed. Only the truth is I can't shift you out of my head. You kept walking there even when I'm asleep.'

'Surely Catherine objects to that if you toss and turn all night,' I said playfully.

'Catherine and I don't ... Mrs Dean keeps a strict eye on that,' he said. 'Not that I would ever insult her by suggesting ... she was brought up very respectable.'

'Not loving beyond reason?'

He shook his head.

The afternoon was wearing on and despite the fire, darkness was insinuating itself into the room, girdling the stairs and the furniture.

'It grows late,' I said. 'I'd best be riding back to the Grange. Mrs Heathcliff and Mrs Dean will be crowing over the materials they've already bought in Leeds. Do you see yourself in black broadcloth? And she will make a model gentleman of you yet I don't doubt! And I will return to Ireland with my commission unperformed.'

'What commission?' he said in a puzzled fashion.

'Mr Heathcliff asked me to visit him here at the house he always called home,' I said. 'Maybe he had a presentiment of his own death but he wanted a great deal for you, Hareton. And he sent you a gift.'

'A gift? With you?'

'Aye,' I said. 'He wanted more for you than you ever wanted for yourself. Will you see to Minty and then come up to the room with the boxbed in it?'

'Aye, I will,' he said slowly.

I took a candle from the dresser and lit it from the fire and went up the staircase and opened the door, seeing the shadows quiver into alertness as I set the candle on the sconce and turned towards the wide bed in which two children had dreamed their dreams and where one of them had died, within sight of his lost Cathy, but restless still.

It was a full fifteen minutes before I heard his step on the stairs and then his tap on the half-closed door.

'Hareton?' I said.

He entered, automatically pushing the door closed behind him and stood looking at me in that place of ruined dreams. His eyes moved from the dark pile of discarded garments on the floor to where I stood, the ruby apples rosy in my ears, the bone ring upon my finger and my black hair unbound flowing under its sheen of red to my waist.

'I am Heathcliff's daughter,' I said. 'I am his gift to you.'

And then he moved forward and he put his arms about me and the candle flame waved a greeting to the past and cast its light over the boxbed and I pleasured him until the candle was melted wax nestling about the spike of the sconce and dawn lit up the sky beyond the lattice window.

EIGHTEEN

'I knew there was something of Mr Heathcliff in you,' Hareton said as we drank tea the following morning. 'Something in the way you hold your head, in the curve of your cheek, but all softened and made female.'

'I have known it for many years,' I said, 'but he would tell me very little of himself. I didn't even know the name of the house where he lived though he invited me to visit him when I was twenty-one. I felt he had no wish to foist me upon Yorkshire until he had laid all his plans.'

'And death interrupted him,' Hareton said.

'Yes, it did.' I too was silent for a spell.

'Well,' Hareton said, putting down his cup and grimacing slightly. 'This puts me in a fair quandary and no mistake. I don't know what to do about it.'

'Oh, I make no claim upon you,' I said quickly. 'I was his gift to you but one is not bound to accept a gift.'

'But I did accept it,' he countered. 'I joyed in the taking of it. All the dreams that have troubled my sleep since you came were solid and real and more beautiful than any dreaming last night. And the odd thing is that it felt right. It felt right and true.'

'For me also,' I said softly, meaning it.

'I don't know what the devil to tell Catherine,' he said at last. 'Will you tell her?'

'I don't know as how I can keep it secret,' he said, the frown on his face a troubled one. 'I'd never, well, you know, and Catherine knows that I never, but when we're wed she'll know then. She's very clever at ferreting things out is Catherine.'

'But she was married before,' I said.

'Linton were dying and she had been forced to it.'

'But she had loved him once,' I reminded him. 'She was alone with him for weeks before his death, you told me. Might she not . . . out of pity?'

'She'd've told me.'

'Why would she? She was on bad terms with you then and for a long while afterwards.'

'She wasn't on any terms at all,' he said. 'She would leave the room if I showed my face. It upset Mr Heathcliff for he was fond of me, but he never showed his feelings much. Oh, when he lost his temper there was no reasoning with him then. I angered him by standing up for her when she put him in a passion. Not that she's cruel, no, I'd not have you think that but she liked to stir things up, to defy him. She liked to stir Joseph up too though the poor old man dared not raise a hand against her. She told him she was a witch who could cast spells and nearly frightened him to death for a day or two.'

'Poor old Joseph!' I said.

'Who'll be starting back this morning and nothing done!' He was on his feet, looking in dismay at the uncleared hearth and the table with its evidence of a guest.

'I'll help you make all right again,' I said briskly. 'You see to the fire and I'll wash these up – and the upstairs room?'

'Oh, I'm the only one ever goes in there now,' Hareton assured me. 'Nelly and Catherine won't set foot in the chamber and neither will Joseph. I'll see to that later.'

'But are you not afraid to enter,' I said, and put up my hand to his cheek where the stubble was beginning to show dark.

'Nay, there's nowt to fear from the dead if you've loved them when they were living,' he said simply, and almost without thinking, or so it seemed to me, took my hand and bit gently into the wrist, leaving a slight, tingling pain that held its own pleasure for me. 'Not that I can remember my aunt Catherine. She never came here after she moved to the Grange. But I've no reason to think she ever wished me ill and Mr Heathcliff always did his best for me, whatever people say.'

'And your mother died,' I said.

'Aye, when I were a few months old. Frances was her name. She was from the south.'

'My mother died when I was born,' I said. I gently freed my hand and began picking up the used cups from the table.

'I never asked about her.'

He went down on one knee and began raking out the spent ashes.

'Her name was Rosina,' I said. 'My grandfather told me she was gentle and sweet with reddish hair. When your aunt decided to wed Edgar Linton he fled from here – Mr Heathcliff I mean – and went to Ireland. My grandfather befriended him and Rosina fell in love with him and consoled him a little for the loss of his true love. He married her for she was a respectable girl but she died at my birthing. Theirs was a spring blossom of a match that faded soon. Like your aunt's with Edgar Linton or—'

'Catherine's with Linton?' he said.

'I was thinking rather of Catherine's with you,' I told him. 'She was alone and lonely and she could not help but see the sweetness of your temper and your wish to console her, so she resolved to make a gentleman of you, but that isn't my business.'

I left him to think over what I had said and went through to the kitchen to rinse out the cups.

He walked through after a few minutes and stood watching me.

'I cannot give her up,' he said at last. 'Oh, I know she sees me as her invention but she's truly fond of me and I . . . Aspen, what we are in ourselves and to each other, we have to forget.'

'I make no claim upon you,' I said simply. 'I came here at my father's bidding, but what I have said and done has been at the request of my own heart and I must bear the pain of that alone. I make no claim upon you or the houses.'

'Houses? What houses?'

'Mr Heathcliff died before making a will so the properties both reverted, Wuthering Heights to you and Thrushcross Grange to her,' I said. 'But I am his legitimate heir. Nobody will know of it. Nobody, Hareton. It only pains me that this house where I feel so much at home will be left to decay as if the people who lived and loved here never existed. But you will be a fine gentleman at the Grange and you will forget me after I return to Ireland.'

'Forget you?' He took a step forward and for an instant I felt myself quail, for the savage temper of the Earnshaws was in his face. 'You talk like a fool. How can I forget myself, Aspen? How can I forget the self within me that rode up to my door and revealed herself to me and gave me back myself in her embraces? How can I forget the scent of you and the bruising nearness of you and the whisper of your voice in the candle-light? You must think me a fool if you imagine I will ever forget you or that the pain of losing you will ever grow less! But this house is yours! You can claim it and stay here if you wish.'

'And have you ride over from the Grange, tea on Sunday with

your black broadcloth suit on and your pretty wife trotting ahead to remind you of your grammar and your manners? I hardly think so!'

'The Grange is yours too,' he said.

'I'll not deprive Catherine of that either,' I flared. 'The two properties are not mine because I will not reveal the truth of my father's marriage and you will say nothing either. It is the only thing I ask of you. Let everything be as it was and let me leave in peace.'

I walked past him to take up my other garments and heard him say, just before I went round to get Minty.

'But how shall I live without myself?'

Did I believe that I would let him choose? I don't know. I only know that as I rode I felt, so clearly in my mind that it might have been happening in reality, his arms about my waist as the pony gathered speed, his breath in my ear, his mouth on my unbound hair.

We passed Penistone Crags and I saw, or thought that I saw, the old woman with the apples on her grey plaits, but it might have been a shadow cast by one of the pointed rocks.

There was a groom waiting to take Minty when I reached the stables and two women chopping up vegetables in the kitchen. They gave me a polite good morning, assuming that I had been out for an early morning gallop, I suppose. I went up to the room from which Isabella Linton had fled and rang for hot water but when it came I merely sponged my hands and face because I wanted the scent of Hareton still on my body and in the folds of my riding habit.

When I came downstairs the girl with the flaxen ringlets stood before the portrait of her brother, casting no reflection in the glass. This time I studied her more minutely, seeing the small, pretty mouth and the blue eyes in which something lingered that was impossible to describe and the hands with their pointed, shining nails. I had the distinct impression that beneath the demure façade lurked a feline creature who would not hesitate to employ her pretty talons to good effect if she were thwarted, and for no reason I can explain found myself thinking, I'd wrench them off her fingers if they ever menaced me.

She drifted out through the door without looking at me and the servant bringing in some food shivered as Isabella's shade passed her by.

'It's turned chilly this morning, Miss Stewart,' she said as she put the dish on the table. 'Shall I get a fire lit for thee?'

'If you wish,' I said indifferently, and thought that no fire would ever warm this splendid house where all the new curtains were up and no doubt a bed made up for the happy wedded pair come New Year's Day.

In the two days that followed I amused myself by going over the house, for no doors had been locked and with the few servants coming and going in the kitchen quarters and only seeing to the rooms I had rented, I was free to explore.

There was a fine library and cases with pretty ornaments set on velvet and displayed through glass and new bright carpets unrolled over the polished floors and clocks ticking monotonously on the mantelshelves.

I imagined Catherine and Hareton returning from their wedding to greet assembled guests though there would be a dearth of blood relatives as they were the last of their line. As I saw too, with a smile tilting the corners of my mouth, that one of the prettiest bedchambers was hung in pink with a fringe of gold silk and that another was furnished in green.

The former had a little closet off it walled with mirrors and a dressing-table supplied with narrow drawers for jewellery and gloves and feminine bobs while the latter had a mahogany tall-boy and a hunting print on the wall.

Linton husbands and wives slept apart and visited by special arrangement then. I couldn't picture Hareton in either of the rooms, nor did I waste much effort in trying. I merely reminded myself that Mr and Mrs Earnshaw had slept apart by the time Heathcliff was brought to the Heights and then I thought of Hugh Brunty and his Ellis, not touching in their bed in their house in Imdel, and I knew that my feelings were not the kind that would ever warm the world. Instead they might extinguish all within reach in fire and flame.

On the third day Catherine rode over with Mrs Dean trudging behind.

'Good morning, Miss Stewart! I apologize again for making such a muddle when you arrived!' she cried when she was shown into the long sitting-room. 'Ah Nelly! There you are! You would not believe it, Miss Stewart, but I have had to walk my horse practically all the way here for Mrs Dean simply cannot keep up!'

'You mean she does not gallop like a horse?' I said. 'How remiss of her.'

'My mistress was joking, Miss Stewart,' Mrs Dean said with a fond glance in the former's direction. 'The walk does me good.'

'Did you have a satisfactory time in Leeds?' I asked, rising to summon tea and biscuits.

'Oh, we bought so much that I feared we'd never get it back,' Catherine said. 'Pale gold for the dress as I think I mentioned and silk flowers, for roses are hard to find in January. You will be in Ireland again by then, or had you thoughts of staying longer in Yorkshire? I fear the inhospitable weather might defeat your intentions.'

'Oh, my plans are very fluid,' I evaded.

'So you leave in mid-December. I hope your business dealings have a satisfactory conclusion.'

'My grandfather's dealings rather,' I said. 'I hope so too.'

The tea and biscuits were brought in and Catherine, having sipped one and taken a few dainty bites of the other, went off upstairs to satisfy herself that the rooms were finished to her satisfaction, I suppose.

'You must be weary,' I said to Mrs Dean.

'A bit,' she admitted. 'Miss Catherine forgets that I am in my forties and get a bit puffed out these days, but she was always a creature of quicksilver, darting here and everywhere like a butterfly. Linton – her other cousin whom she married first – was never able to keep up with her for she was always urging him to be more energetic, not really understanding that his illness made it hard for him. But I've not liked staying alone at the Heights since Mr Heathcliff died and Joseph is over in the village collecting for some heathen charity or other and Hareton went over to Sowdons so I came over here with my little lady.'

'How is Mr Earnshaw?' I asked.

'A bit off-colour,' she admitted. 'Nervous about the wedding like all bridegrooms I suppose. I shall be glad when it's over and we're settled here.'

I said nothing and she went on to chat about a few trivialities until Catherine tripped down the stairs again.

'Such happy memories this house holds for me,' she said. 'I was hardly ever beyond the grounds save with papa until I was thirteen years old and I knew nothing of Wuthering Heights or my cousins there. Papa wished to protect me from that evil man whose name I absolutely refuse to pronounce in this house! Nelly, are you ready?'

'As soon as you are,' Mrs Dean said fondly.

'Oh, I almost forgot! Nelly, you ought to have reminded me. I left it in the passage!'

She went out and returned with a large square parcel done up with string.

'My mother's portrait,' she said. 'I never knew her of course but they say it's very like her. Mr . . . that evil man took it to the Heights when poor papa died and would allow nobody to look at it but his own selfish eyes and since his death it's been in that awful bedchamber where . . . anyway, I brought it over to hang in its old place next to Papa's picture but it will require cleaning before that. And the backing is starting to peel away too. Everything decays at Wuthering Heights! Have you been to Penistone Crags? One can see the Heights and this house from up there and this house is by far the better residence though Hareton hates to admit it! Nelly, are you ready? Miss Stewart, we must leave. I am glad to find you comfortable here but I must admit that I shall be delighted when I am in possession of it again. Nelly, come!'

She flitted out, Mrs Dean obediently behind, and the parcel leaning against the wall.

When they had gone, Mrs Dean having got her second wind, gamely keeping up with her mounted mistress, I stood in the stable and leaned my head for a moment against Minty's side as the emptiness and silence of the place, save for the occasional mutterings of the servants in the kitchen, folded itself about me like a shroud.

I would ride to the crags, I decided, and see two different worlds in two different directions. I might also see the gypsy woman though I regarded that as unlikely.

I dawdled through my toilet, calculating how long it would take them to arrive at the Heights for I'd no desire to have Catherine point out its beauties as if the crags were her own private property, and then I donned a plain riding-dress of dark red and left my hair to blow in the rising wind as I mounted Minty.

The wind was stronger than I had imagined, tearing at the edges of my cloak, whipping up the waters of the beck. The sun

214

still cast its gold over the topmost peaks leaving the rocks beneath in shadow and as I neared the shingled path that twisted upwards, I fancied for a moment I saw two shadows clasped together on the little spot of level ground from where I had seen Hareton and Catherine on that first occasion.

I was mistaken. When I reached that spot I beheld a solitary horse tethered to a thorn bush and no person in sight.

I knew he was there. I knew it in my bones and my blood and I dismounted and tethered Minty next to the other and began the long slow walk up to the great flat rock at the summit with the entrance to the fairy cave opening like a bud in the gold-flecked stone.

Hareton was within, in the place where the entrance with its low roof rose up into a cave with tiny stones and tufts of wild-flowers embedded in the rock and the ground strewn with grasses blown there over the preceding months. The cave itself wasn't dark but shadowed gently with shafts of light arrowing in through gaps high in the roof.

Hareton lay there. He was weeping softly as if he feared to disturb the tiny insects that ploughed the moss that clung to the rockface or the long thin skeins of cobweb that swayed against the slits between the stones. His back was bare and I could see the redness still on his arm and the half-healed scar where he had tripped over his fowling piece and received a sprinkling of buckshot.

I bent beneath the entrance and sat by him, stroking his back almost as I might quiet a quivering animal and he twisted about, sat up and choked back a sob as he said, 'Before God, Aspen, I don't know what's best to be done! I am so fond of Catherine. I was so proud when she stopped insulting me and began to see me as a human being with feelings and a mind, and she's been so patient in helping with my reading and the writing and the figuring, and she is so sweet and pretty and has had such ill usage since her father died; I cannot tell what's best to be done!'

'You must do as your heart bids,' I said.

'My heart can scarcely beat for the weight that's upon it,' he said and leaned forward, putting his hands in my unbound hair and pulling the black strands through his fingers.

'I will not deprive you or Catherine of your properties,' I assured him. 'Hareton, I would never have come to you but it was the last wish of my father. He thought so much of you! He had plans for your betterment.'

'I knew it but Catherine insisted that he had no plans save to leave me ignorant,' he said and eagerness had leapt into his voice.

'And she will not have his name mentioned at Thrushcross Grange,' I said sadly.

'And she will not live at the Heights. I cannot blame her for she was always unhappy there. The Grange is her home.'

'She is a Linton,' I said, and sat back on my heels, my eyes downcast, my hair still tangled in his fingers.

'Her mother was an Earnshaw,' he said.

'Who chose to become a Linton. Hareton, if you love her then you will be living as a Linton, and you will surely be happy to have a fine house in a great park and the best society—'

'I choose my own society,' he said, and loosed my hair so abruptly that I almost fell.

'And I will return to Ireland,' I said. 'The marriage that Mr Heathcliff made will remain a secret.'

'And I will seek you in every face I see,' he said and his face was dark with fury. 'I will dream of you when I sleep and hunger for you when I wake and for the rest of my life live separated from myself. And the Heights where once I knew some content even in the bad times will crumble into nothingness and the moors will be desolate save for the ghosts who roam there.'

'It will be better so,' I said soberly. 'Goodbye, Hareton.'

I rose, pushing back my hair and he sat there, his head bowed for a moment, one hand plucking at the moss. Then he said, in a voice that woke echoes in my mind, 'I wish someone would hold me just for a moment.'

And I knelt down and held him and time was not.

NINETEEN

'So you will be leaving before your rental period is over?' Mrs Dean said.

I had gone into the village to arrange for the booking of a seat on the coach and to enquire the times of embarkation at Liverpool.

She was just emerging from one of the small shops and looked pleased to see me, though that was simply, I quickly discovered, because she saw the time when she would live again at the Grange with her ewe-lamb and husband as drawing ever nearer.

'My business here is finished sooner than I expected,' I said. 'I will, of course, not ask for any reduction on the rent I've paid.'

'Of course not,' she agreed. 'My Miss Catherine will take nothing less. So you will be in Ireland again for Christmas?'

'Where the weather will be somewhat milder, I hope!' I said.

'Aye, this country breeds tough people,' she said with a smile. 'The weak go under here.'

But not until they have destroyed the strong, I thought, and remembered what she had told me about Hindley Earnshaw whose wife's death had driven him to the bottle, and Linton Heathcliff whose ill health had expressed itself in petty spite to disappoint his father.

'You will not mention that you and I talked?' She seemed to divine my thoughts for she put her hand on my arm to detain me a moment longer.

'I will keep your confidences,' I said.

'And you'll call at the Heights to say goodbye?'

'Yes,' I said, and wondered why I should seek to torture myself. Had Mr Heathcliff felt as I felt when he had his final meeting with his Cathy?

'I must get on. I've other errands to run,' she said. 'I shall tell my little lady that you will call before you leave.'

And that would be the end of it all. I would ride up to the old house Hareton thought of as his home and shake hands with his pretty Catherine and wish her joy in her marriage and leave, I doubted I would see Hareton at all. I think in that moment I silently cursed my father for dying before I came into Yorkshire.

I wondered too if I would ever glimpse Mr Heathcliff and his Cathy again, restless even in death because the tale was not wound up and the miseries he had suffered and the cruelties he had inflicted stayed unresolved, the weak preying on the strong.

I walked Minty down the lane past the parson's house. The small garden if such a name could be justified was empty and the wind blew over the wall and the gravestones beyond almost as fiercely as it blew about Wuthering Heights and Penistone Crags.

Past the stile I mounted up and set my course for the Grange. The skies were ice grey and the grass beneath Minty's hoofs drained of colour like the world in which I soon would dwell. I would not see Hareton again for his own good heart had led him into rejecting what we had shared. I would not show the marriage lines of Mr Heathcliff and Rosina Stewart to Mrs Dean's little lady. The Grange was silent save for the subdued chatter of two women washing up in the kitchen.

I went into the back quarters and told them I wouldn't

require them any longer that evening, that on the next day my bags would be collected and I would leave Minty at the inn at Gimmerton for the owner to take.

And then I walked through the cool, empty, elegant rooms. A fire had been lit in the long sitting-room which gave light but no real heat. Upstairs not a breath disturbed the neat chambers with their pristine hangings and thick carpets and dainty ornaments on velvet under glass.

Hareton would no more give up Catherine for me than her mother had deserted Edgar Linton for my father. The mating of souls had nothing to do with marriage.

And Mr Heathcliff had lost the last tangible reminder of his only true love, for the portrait of Catherine Earnshaw had been taken from the room they had once shared and brought to the Grange again to hang beside the portrait of her lawful husband, blue-eyed, fair-haired Edgar Linton.

It still leaned against the wall, the backing peeling away, the proud passionate eyes hidden. I stepped over and took it up, sat on the sofa and began to release it from its bindings.

The paper was old and tore easily, layer after layer coming to pieces in my hands. I sat down with the wadding strewn about my feet and turned the portrait to face me, seeing in the amber-glinted eyes the eyes of Hareton, tracing his more masculine features in her face.

'You betrayed Heathcliff for money and position,' I said aloud and something in the room stirred and shivered at my words.

Then I stood up, hung the portrait next to its companion, bent to pick up the discarded wadding.

The document was rolled neatly between two shielding squares of cardboard. My fingers unrolled it and held it a little nearer to the lamp that stood on the small table nearby.

It was written in a bold, flowing hand and dated the twenty-first of March in this year.

I, Heathcliff, being in sound body and mind, and having legally in my possession the properties of Wuthering Heights and Thrushcross Grange, do will and bequeath the said properties together with the livestock and income derived thereof as follows.

To Hareton Earnshaw, my foster nephew, the land and building known as Wuthering Heights on condition he retains it as his principal residence.

To Catherine Heathcliff, widow of my son, Linton Heathcliff, the land and buildings known as Thrushcross Grange on condition she never marries Hareton Earnshaw. Should she not abide by this injunction the said property shall revert to Aspen Stewart, my legal daughter by Rosina Stewart, deceased, of Imdel, Northern Ireland.

To my daughter, the said Aspen, I leave the income derived from my Dublin business and charge Mr G. Alistair, Attorney at Law, with the handling and distribution of all profits from the said business.

A copy of this aforewritten will has been dispatched to the said G. Alistair with my instructions that it shall be opened and read should my daughter, Aspen, have the wit to find this.

It was signed by Mr Heathcliff and witnessed by two people I did not know.

I do believe that I laughed aloud then for Mr Heathcliff must have felt his eagerly awaited death approaching, must have known that I would visit the Heights, must have reckoned on an unseen force that would guide me to its discovery.

I imagined him in that upper chamber, knowing that the son and daughter of his most hated enemies were beginning to observe each other with less than hostile eyes, knowing that his Cathy's daughter would give up anything, anyone in order to return to the Grange and that Hareton, though an Earnshaw, would never betray anyone's affection even for the sake of his old home.

It would be Nelly Dean's little lady who would forsake Hareton for her rural palace where she had once lived in peace and luxury.

And that was yesterday. Last night I slept with the rolled document beneath my pillow and my hand clutching it lest some pale ghost glided in to snatch it away, and this afternoon, having spent the morning in writing to Mr Alistair to give him my instructions as to the opening of the letter left with him by Mr Heathcliff, I am ready to ride over to the Heights.

I wear my red habit and my hair is unbound. I ride Minty and inform the woman who has come to do the weekly washing that I will be at the Grange for one more night and then may repair to the inn at Gimmerton.

On my way I pass as usual Penistone Crags and glance towards it. There is a woman there, not the grey-haired crone with the apples in her plaits, but a very small woman, no bigger than a child, clad in a black mourning frock and bonnet, her square plain face redeemed by the beautiful hazel eyes she casts briefly in my direction. She has a little spade with her and is digging a hole in the turf near the shadowing rocks.

At her side, as she kneels there under the grey sky, a manuscript flutters its pages in the wind that sweeps down from the moors. And I have the oddest notion that when the manuscript is buried and the turf sods laid over it and trodden down, I myself will cease to exist as if all along I have been a ghost among ghosts haunting lonely spaces.

I ride on without looking back and Catherine is at the front door, her voice playfully scolding.

'What is the point of cleaning and tidying the upper room when nobody will ever sleep there again? We have to see the Reverend Charnock today to arrange the hymns for the nuptials. And I will not endure the Gimmerton town band blaring their instruments all over the place. I think we shall procure better musicians if we enquire further afield.'

I leaned to unbar the gate and trot in, taking the rolled document from my sleeve.

'I have something for you and Mr Earnshaw to peruse,' I say.

'Not a complaint about the rent I hope,' she says, sweetly playful.

'A copy of Mr Heathcliff's will,' I tell her. 'I have the original in my possession and other copies are with my lawyer in Ireland.'

Hareton is standing on the stairs, his lambent dark eyes fixed upon me like a man starving who sees nourishment arrive just out of his reach. And because I cannot be absolutely sure of Catherine's final answer I look back at him as if I were a soul sighting heaven with a barred gate in the way.

'That man never left a will!' she says sharply.

'If you will read it – both of you – then you will see that he did,' I say. 'He tried to make all right at the end. He was always good to Hareton you know.'

'Hareton?' She looks at me and at him and something flashes into her dark eyes, recognition perhaps.

'I will be at the inn at Gimmerton tomorrow,' I say. 'You can inform me of your decision then.'

And I look past her to where Hareton stands, drink in his dark beauty and hold his own imploring, hungry gaze before I turn my mount and canter off down the slopes again.

It grows darker now, storm clouds rushing in to throw veils of smoky grey and purple over the remaining light. I have had one swift, upward glance at the latticed window of the room where the boxbed dominates and have glimpsed for an instant the two dark children standing there, so close that they appear almost as one.

Near the peat marsh on the edge of the moor I draw rein and dismount, tethering Minty to a thorn tree, and I walk, my cloak and my hair blowing in the wind, to where three headstones mark the graves of three people. Catherine Linton, née Earnshaw, who betrayed her own self and wed her summer love; Edgar Linton who married his one true love and held her body with his fine house and possessions but never grasped her soul; Heathcliff, parentage uncertain, desolate in a world that had stolen his Cathy and that with her willing consent, seeking the daughter who might have understood him.

I kneel on the ground and place my hands, palm down, on the hard earth that covers him as the heavy stone at Imdel covers my mother and I whisper into the wind, 'I have loved the very bones of you so much that it hurts my heart, and I will go on loving you until past the ending of time. Sleep now and all will go well in the morning.'